A Shadow Over Shanghai

西 東

by
David Keyes

A Cecil Herbert Woolley Mystery

THE HOUSE OF POMEGRANATES PRESS

Published by The House of Pomegranates Press
www.houseofpomegranates.ca
ISBN 978-1-7751808-5-2

This book is a work of fiction. Names, characters, places and incidents either
are the products of the author's imagination or are used fictitiously, and any
resemblance to actual persons living or dead, events or locales is entirely
coincidental.

Set in Adobe Garamond Pro and
ITC Luna Com

Garamond is an old style serif typeface originally cut by
Glaude Garamond for the Parisian scholar-printer Robert Estienne in the first part of
the sixteenth century. The Garamond font used in the text of this book was designed by
Robert Slimbach for Adobe Systems in 1989.
ITC Luna is the work of Japanese designer Akira Kobayashi who was inspired by the
designs of the 1930s.

Designed in 2019 by Gillian Holmes of
The House of Pomegranates Press
and typeset in Toronto on an iMac computer.
Copyedited by Jean Nielsen.

For Gillian, the patron saint of lost causes

A
Shadow
Over
Shanghai

The mistress of the house put her hand on his shoulder. Woolley could only make out the glint of gold in her teeth and the yellowy white of her eyes in the dull, cloudy candlelight. "Mr. Woolley, I never say this to anyone, but maybe you should find some other way to not dream. To people who walk with ghosts, the pipe only brings them demons." She turned and quietly said something in Malay dialect to the shadows. A very young girl in an orange silk cheongsam appeared balancing a tray with a small black cup and an earthen pot of tea that smelled remarkably of a barnyard. "You drink this and sleep, you will be safe, I watch you. I wake you when it time to go home. I like you Mr. Woolley, but maybe you no come back."

Chapter 1

He came to. Someone was shaking him, "Sir, Sir…"

"Not now," he mumbled, not wanting to leave. "Benedict? Benedict, you're not supposed to be here." He felt a violent shudder; they were coming. "Steady on old man!" he shouted.

"Oh, for god 's sake," a woman's voice suddenly said. "Cecil, wake up…" and a glass of ice water was poured onto his face, waking him rudely.

He opened his eyes painfully and there before him was Clemency. "Have I died? " he muttered. "Am I in heaven, are you an angel?"

"Oh, for goodness' sake Cecil," Clemency said, irritably. "You lost three games of Uncle Wiggly and drank most of a bottle of gin. We are on a train, we are in Siberia, it is tomorrow — early evening as a matter of fact — and those nice men you see on the platform in the rather attractive coats, large hats carrying rather enormous guns will soon be here in this cabin wanting to see our travel papers…."

Chapter 2

"*What charming young* men," said Clemency, putting her papers back in their protective sleeve.

"I didn't like the look of that one with the moustache; he seemed rather shifty."

"Oh darling, he looked about 18."

"You can be shifty at any age. I've known shifty babies. And I didn't like the way he poked me with his gun." Cecil smoothed down his clothes with the flat of his hands then righted his tie in the reflection of the window. "Any chance of getting a drink? I suppose it's just vodka from here on in."

There was a knock on the door.

Woolley smiled at Clemency. "Expecting someone, darling?"

"Perhaps that lovely young man with the moustache."

"I'll have him stripped of his rank if he so much as places a hand ... ah, it's Benedict."

Benedict entered carrying a tray with a bucket of ice, a shaker, two cocktail glasses, a small glass of olives and a bottle of Gordon's Gin. He placed the tray on the small pull-down table by the window. "I took the liberty of be-friending the Mongolian bar staff during the inspection;

they were happy to allow me the use of tray and shaker. A drink, sir? Madam?"

"Benedict, you are a saint, a saint. You speak Mongolian?"

"Only enough to make sure my mutton is not warmed in a boodog. And I am hardly a saint, sir, but thank you." Benedict poured four shots of Gordon's into the shaker. He then tipped a soupçon of olive juice from the glass and added seven irregularly-shaped ice cubes. Woolley felt something akin to absolute love as Benedict then shook the concoction: five strokes forward, three side-to-side, then five forward. Clemency watched the two men lost in the ritual and smiled. Benedict uncapped the shaker and poured the drink into each glass. Slivers of ice floated on top like chips of precious diamonds. Woolley handed a glass to Clemency and then took up his own. "Darling. To friends no longer with us!"

Clemency smiled again, "Absent friends." They both drank.

"Lord … Benedict, that is simply the best dirty martini I've ever had. Was it the motion of the train that added to the effervescence?"

Benedict began preparing a second cocktail. "I cannot say, sir. Practice and concentration. Dinner will be served in the forward car at seven. I have reserved you and Miss de la Tour a private table. You will be expected. If there is not anything else…?"

"No, nothing, Benedict. How are you doing? Well set up?"

"I am sharing my cabin with a young gentleman of the theatrical profession. A magician from the East, I believe. The conversation, what little there's been, has been most interesting."

"Excellent, excellent. You must glean some tricks."

"I will do my best, sir," Benedict said, pouring out the second drink.

Clemency sipped. "Thank you, Benedict. I don't think we'll need anything else for tonight."

"Yes, Benedict, do have the rest of the night. Are you still Proust-ing?"

"No sir, I had to put it aside. I'm now moving between *Winnie the Pooh* and *The Story of the Eye*."

Clemency put down her glass. "Have you read *Orlando* yet? I simply loved that, and I generally do not like that woman."

"And I've just put down Montague Summers' new tome about Vampires and their bally kin," said Woolley. "That man is a stick. Must be the religion in him... stiffens you." He drained his drink. "What a book club we are!"

"Oh, Woolley," Clemency said as she slipped her hand into his and kissed him.

"Darling," Woolley sighed as he kissed her back.

Benedict gathered up the tray and glasses and left the cabin.

Clemency turned and put her arms around Woolley, placing her feet on top of his. He slowly waltzed her around the cabin. "I could get used to this," he said, kissing her once more.

A voice bellowed from the corridor, "обед подан! Dîner est servi! 晚餐供應! Dinner is served!"

With her lips pressed to his, Clemency said, "I am

assuming dinner is served."

"In four languages, no less."

Clemency climbed off Woolley's feet, catching their reflection in the black glass of the train window. Woolley was dressed in a grey loose suit, a maroon tie, a gold clasp and matching maroon pocket square; Clemency was in a black shift dress with beading that shimmered, her skin pale white against the black.

"Are we decent for dinner?" asked Woolley.

"More than decent."

"And you, darling … divine. Absolute perfection."

Clemency kissed him. "Help me find my shoes."

Chapter 3

Cecil opened the cabin door to let Clemency out, then followed into the dimly lit corridor. He turned and locked the door. The long passage was lined on one side with polished cabin doors, on the other windows and ornate wood panelling burnished to a warm glow. The minimal lighting was from wall sconces with red shades. The windows, black from the night, were frosted from the cold air. Blue velvet curtains hung and swayed with the motion of the train. It seemed as one revolution ended, another more bloody and unrelenting started up. The country was righting wrongs, bringing itself into the 20th century, but what little gain was hard fought and hard won. The past did not want to let go. In the long golden hallways of the palaces, the ghosts that had wandered for millennia did not want to leave.

Woolley unclasped a window and slid it down. Instantly a cold gust of air blew in. "What a place in which to be friendless, " he said and turned to Clemency. "Clemency, darling, thank you."

"For what, darling?"

He took her in his arms, "For being perfect, perfectly perfect to me."

"Oh Woolley, honestly, when you say such things I think you really don't know me at all. How could you think me perfect? I'm an average girl."

"Ha! Average! Shall I make a list, starting with your lovely brain and ending with your lovely bottom? And no girl can be said 'average' who is somehow related to the secret service and loaded. Let's not forget that. Loaded."

Clemency kissed Woolley. "It is my money, isn't it — my assets?"

"Absolutely not. I would love you if you were penniless, a beggar girl. You were made to be loved by a lost misfit like me. We are misfits, darling. Let's hope there's an excellent wine list!"

Just then a small man in a white dinner jacket pushed by in a hurry. "Excuse," he grunted as an afterthought.

"Extraordinary," said Woolley, frowning and letting go of Clemency while pausing to appreciate the feel of her bare breasts moving beneath the fabric of her dress. "There is a fellow with indigestion."

"He vaguely resembled a bug, wouldn't you agree?"

"Not a nice bug," said Woolley, "not nice." People are in such a hurry these days, he thought. How can one be in a hurry when they are on a journey of 9,259 kilometers that takes eight days to complete? There's nothing really to hurry to except perhaps the bar car and the hope of food that doesn't still have eyes left in it. Woolley pushed up the window and with a gesture, encouraged Clemency forward.

They wound their way along the corridor hesitantly, as the rocking of the train was quite pronounced. Outside the train they caught a shimmer; they looked out to see squares of orange light, small houses, and further off the glow of large fires burning. Clemency shivered. "A festival?"

"A revolution, more than likely. From now on we must be very mindful of what we say and who we talk to."

"Oh Woolley, is it that bad?"

"I fear it may be, darling. But let us focus on the food and drink before us, and the fact that you and I are gloriously alone on a magical train, warm and in love as we speed through the chilly Siberian night."

Clemency smiled and slipped her hand into Woolley's, gripping it tightly. They kissed. More passengers jostled by. Women in traditional costumes, women in elegant dresses and feathers, men in dinner jackets, many in military garb, each acknowledging the couple in their own way.

"I fear we've become a spectacle," said Clemency.

"Wherever we go, my darling, wherever we go."

They shifted down the carpeted way, eventually reaching the coupling section. Woolley cracked the door and they were hit with an instant explosion of sound and cold. "Lord!" shouted Woolley to Clemency as he quickly pushed the adjacent door and hurried Clemency through. They entered a warm vestibule with more varnished wood and a door with a window of peacocks etched in the glass. Through that was the dining car. The smell of food and cigarette smoke was intoxicating.

"Shall we?" asked Woolley.

"Yes, let's." Clemency replied, and they slid the door aside.

The dining car was lush and overheated, half full of glistening patrons. The decorating scheme was suffocated with ornamentation. Gold everywhere. On the ceiling were polished wooden beams with garish patterns in between, and atop the purple velvet plush backs dividing the booths was curling metal work. Each table was lit by a small deco lamp, dangling crystals swaying with the rhythm of the train, and had a small fluted silver vase. Crisp white tablecloths and a patterned carpet that looked of trampled-upon ikons. There was a smattering of tourists, some army officers and a few men who looked all business. The whole gave the impression of a bought second-hand hotel restaurant. Everything made on the cheap, everything lacking that luster that said it was well made, the carpet frayed at the edges, the booths worn, lumpy and ill upholstered. Woolley turned to Clemency, "Brings to mind Teignmouth in South Devon where I acquired food poisoning."

Clemency tittered, "Charming."

An unnaturally thin, pale and pomaded maître' d in an opulent train uniform approached with menus.

"I am Woolley, I believe my man reserved…."

"Mr. Woolley!" purred the man. "No need to introduce, your table is here. I've held the best for you." Then, turning and giving Clemency a wink, "right by the bar."

"Excellent, excellent."

He guided them to their table and put down two menus and a wine list. "The cellar is quite good, sir."

"Worries me a little," smiled Clemency as they settled into the booth.

"What does, darling?"

"He said, 'Our cellar is quite good.' Can you imagine some poor cabin boy having to shimmy down there for some of the 1878?"

Cecil snorted and considered the menu. "Interesting translations here. I will avoid the intestinal chicken – you?"

"Same for the pork eyes. Lord, what could that be?! Not really. Do you think?"

"Should we order them?" smiled Woolley.

"No!"

A waiter in a lesser version of the maître' d's uniform (less frog, more stains) appeared by their table, pressing himself against the edge for balance. "Would you like something to drink?" he said in a thick, unrecognizable accent.

Cecil smiled – foolish question. "I'm assuming it's vodka from here on in?"

The waiter clicked his heals. "No sir, we also have a number of gins, English gins."

"Ah. Darling? A martini to refuel, take stock, etc.?"

"Oh, absolutely."

"Two icy, dry gin martinis please, shook, olives. Thank you. Then, while we're drinking we'll think about eating. Sound good to you darling?"

"Cecil?"

"Clemency?"

"I've never been more in love."

Suddenly without warning the train ground to a sudden, horrific, screeching halt. The sound of crashing dishes and cutlery was deafening. Many languages and dialects loudly brought to the fore a myriad of deities. The waiter fell back and hit the floor hard. Woolley shot up to offer his assistance. "No, no, please," said the waiter smoothing his uniform with one hand, his hair with the other. "I am quite used to these disturbances."

Clemency pulled the cutlery from her lap and placed it back on the table. "What could it be, I wonder?" she asked, looking out at the black night and seeing only her own reflection. In the distance there were three brief flashes of light.

"Ah," said the waiter.

"Ah? That meant something to you?" questioned Woolley.

"A rebel has been shot, probably found on the train by the guards and chased off. That was gunfire. I'm sure he is dead now. We can move on."

Cecil looked at Clemency and frowned. "A rebel?"

"Yes," said the waiter, righting the vase that had toppled and mopping up the water. "They are vermin." The train jostled and began to move.

"But what will become of him?" asked Clemency.

The waiter leaned forward to straighten the tablecloth and said, "The wolves will dine well tonight." Then, changing his tone, "It is not of your concern. They are not really people. I will get you your drinks," and walked away.

Clemency nervously picked up the silver vase. "What a lovely blue flower," she said.

"Siberian squill, late this year," said Woolley.

Clemency smiled and reached for a cigarette. Woolley leaned over and lit it. She couldn't help but notice his hand was shaking.

Chapter 4

With drinks ordered, Clemency cast her gaze out of the window. "Oh Woolley, what is this place?"

"End of the old gods, start of the new. Kicking and screaming."

"Quite right Mr. Woolley," said the large man in a breathy, gravelly voice from the booth beside them. "Forgive me," he continued. "Let me introduce myself. Moffatt St. Andrew Woodside-Chang. It is an honour to finally meet you." He moved his head as in a bow, losing his chin into the folds of his neck. "And you must be Miss Clemency de la Tour, an honour also." With great delicacy he raised a teacup with his enormous hand as a kind of toast, his movements accentuated by a strong scent of patchouli.

Cecil took him in but could not place him. He resembled a large amphibious creature stuffed into a well-tailored suit. "I can't say we've met before, forgive me, have we?"

"No sir, I only know you from reputation, your war record of course speaks for itself. But I've been fascinated by your work, especially in the occult, for some time. You have not heard of me?"

"I confess I have not, I apologize."

The man made a small moue of discontent, "I concern myself mostly with the East. The western Occult I find is only interested in bickering, cliché, rebellion, profit and scandal. Perhaps you've heard of the Order of the Golden Dawn? Yes?" He paused dramatically and dipped his bejewelled hand into a bowl of rose water. "The H.B. of L., the Hermetic Brotherhood of Luxor?"

Woolley smiled, the drinks had arrived. He watched with anticipation as the waiter delicately placed the frosted glass in front of him. After the server had retreated Woolley held up one finger and taking the glass, sipped. He smiled again, "Ah."

Moffatt St. Andrew Woodside-Chang chortled. Clemency frowned. Woolley visibly came back into himself, breathed in and began, "The Golden Dawn, why of course, you were a member? The second order, I am guessing." Woolley assumed the man was lying.

Woodside-Chang settled back and smiled, "I was a sub-imperator tasked to gather wisdom from the East. My mother is English, my father Cantonese. I was born in Macau but educated in England. Eton, Oxford, cruelty, isolation, depression, buggery." He waved his hands as if pushing away a dark cloud. "My parents died by mysterious circumstances when I was at Oxford." He paused for dramatic effect. "Perhaps you've read my paper on The Lost Canon of Proportions of the Egyptians? No? No matter." Again, he waved his hand. "People do not want the math, they want the romance, the mystery." Splotches of red began to form on his face as he made a fist and shook it. "The violence."

"Quite!" said Woolley, settling into his drink. Clemency sipped hers and under the table kicked Woolley.

"I was devastated by the death of my parents. I loved them both … deeply. But with their passing came a great light, a small fortune, shares in a tin mine, which allowed me to … do what I like, as they say. Esoterica was my obsession, the dark arts, alchemy. With this freedom I could pursue these interests without distraction. I took a house in London and began my great work."

The waiter arrived. Woolley signalled another drink. Clemency, sensing a long night, decided to pace herself. "A mineral water, please."

"But of course," said the waiter. "And your food?"

"Ah, we are still considering…"

"Stay away from the meat," Woodside-Chang said. "It's not what they say. Keep to the fish, at least I think it's fish."

The waiter frowned.

Woolley smiled, "I'll have the fish."

"And the lady?"

Clemency snapped shut the menu. "The same. Will there be vegetables?"

"Cabbage, carrots and beets," replied the waiter.

Woodside-Chang chuffed.

Woolley smiled and passed the waiter his empty glass. "I'm sure it will all be excellent." He turned to St. Andrew Woodside-Chang. "And so in London you found your kind, people who thought like you?"

"Ha!" the man barked loudly. Startled, Clemency dropped the fork she was fiddling with. "My own kind! Charlatans! They knew nothing of the hermetic order, nothing of the ways of the elders! They were imposters, bowing down to celebrities, letting anyone in who could pay the dues. My own kind!" He ruminated, "Ha! Like life, like everything, the great religions, the great prophecies, it all started with a lie."

"Ah, so were you able to learn anything from them?" asked Woolley, clearly enjoying himself.

"I learned to watch my ways, to trust only what I learn myself. These adepts, these so-called seers, they were all fools. I took what I could and then moved on. I read their books, slept with their wives." He paused, making sure he had shocked, and seeing he hadn't, continued, "Oh yes, sex magik … so important to those English prudes. They published *The Mystery of Eros* and tried to recruit married couples to, ahem, copulate while they danced about in some half-understood mystical energy. So English, making the servants do the work…" He paused. He had become visibly agitated and the violent red splotches on his face had turned to a solid coating of vermillion.

Woolley was amused, Clemency appalled.

Woodside-Chang took out a large handkerchief and wiped his wet brow. Taking a sip of tea, he wheezed. "I do apologize, we are in a dining car, traveling across the vast and haunted tundra of Siberia. We are not in some English salon arguing like school children. I apologize." His voice trailed off. "As you can see, these matters matter much to me."

Woolley smiled. The second drink had come. "My dear sir, without passion there is no forward, no, ah, thrust." He looked at Clemency, who frowned. "I do understand. But I sense there is disappointment to this story."

"I learned nothing. An Oxfordshire vicar with a science kit in his basement looking for the Philosopher's Stone. Nudists and madmen all saying they know the way. Bosh and nonsense. But I had to see if perhaps they did have some truth, some golden knowledge. After working my way through all their rituals, I came to the realization they had none. Like all the great religions, they were just making it up. The sublime arrives, as Mr. Burke wrote, when religion begins its retreat." He closed his eyes and inhaled dramatically. He opened them and smiled. "Perhaps I was a little too radical for them. I do not pretend to be a comfort..." He laughed, then made eye contact with Clemency, and said very quietly, "I am a curse!"

"Oh dear," Clemency said, again kicking Woolley under the table.

"Yes, well, let us hope you do not curse us fellow travellers," replied Woolley.

"Mr. Woolley, you have me wrong! I find you far and above most of my supposed 'kind'. You are a pioneer, I could learn from you."

Woolley didn't like the sound of that.

The waiter arrived with their order. The fish could have been some sort of bass, Woolley wasn't sure, and as promised, it was surrounded by cabbage, beets and carrots expertly arranged. The plates were lovely and large, printed with the logo of the train line – a scrolling text of T.S.E. intertwined. As the purple of the beet juice ran into the fish portion, Clemency could not but feel foreboding. St. Andrew Woodside-Chang sat back in his booth and lit a brown cheroot, keeping his eyes fixed on Clemency. Settling back, he exhaled a swirl of acrid blue smoke into the air. "So, Mr. Woolley, what brings you to the East ?"

Woolley was fishing fish bone out of the white meat with extreme concentration. "Pleasure, as Oscar Wilde said. What should bring anyone anywhere?"

Woodside-Chang leaned forward and smiled. "Come, come Mr. Woolley, you can't expect me to believe that. You of all people, travelling to a place that at the moment is so dangerous for an Englishman that even your embassy has advised against visiting. Surely you are here on business."

Clemency was now finding menace in everything that St. Andrew Woodside-Chang said. She wanted to leave and was about to kick Woolley again when he kicked her first. She squeaked.

Woolley put down his fork. "It is a simple holiday…. Seeing the sights, visiting old friends, attending to some matters."

"Ah! Then not just for pleasure," enthused Woodside-Chang, clapping his large fleshy hands.

Clemency did not want to talk further with Woodside-Chang staring at her as he was.

He chortled with glee. "Let me guess… you meddled where you should not have. You opened a portal, you angered a spirit."

Woolley pounded his knife down upon the table. "Good god man, not everything is of the spirit." Woolley was visibly angry, a rarely seen state to Clemency. She reached out and put her hand on his. "I am sorry darling…the war…," he said quietly

St. Andrew Woodside-Chang bowed. "I, too, am sorry. I played Pandora and I apologize. I was too ill to fight in that horrific conflict, and I must be more sensitive to the feelings ..."

"No," Woolley interrupted, "you did not know, and it is fine." Woolley took a drink and frowned. Water. He signalled the waiter, held up his martini glass and made a sweeping gesture which the waiter assumed meant, 'keep them coming.' Ominously the lights in the dining car dimmed, went out and then came back on. Clemency would forever be haunted by the vision of St. Andrew Woodside-Chang's huge greasy face glowing in the orange light of his cheroot.

Chapter 5

Having returned to their cabin Clemency felt safe for the first time since meeting Woodside-Chang. "What a dreadful man," she shivered.

Woolley was concentrating on Clemency's behind as she shimmied out of her dress. Her silk camisole, oh so translucent and clinging, was also giving Woolley no end of distraction. "Woolley!"

"Darling, I am here."

"Shanghai … the war … you have never mentioned this before."

"I spent some time there. It was a dark time for me. I have few fond memories but if it weren't for my dear friend's family I would not be here today, this chap that you love."

There was a knock on the door. "Benedict, sir." Clemency hastily put on her robe. Woolley, who was re-clining on the already made-up bed reached out with his foot and flicked up the latch. Benedict entered carrying a tray with a shaker of pre-mixed drinks and a bowl filled with what looked like rusks and pickles. He placed it on the table by the window. "I took the liberty of making your beds while you were dining. Did you find the meal satisfactory?"

"Thank you, Benedict, it was … what word would you give it, Clem?"

"It wasn't that bad at all really," said Clemency, "just slightly off due to the company."

"Ah yes, I enquired about the gentleman sitting next to you, Mr. Moffatt St. Andrew Woodside-Chang. An interesting character."

"Yes?" said Woolley, reaching for the shaker.

"Curious sort really. I happened upon a few students of the occult in my section of the train and they knew of his presence. Insisted I carry this," he pulled out a charm, "to ward off his evil eye. My understanding is that he is English more than anything else and I cannot imagine a foreign charm would be of much use, but I took it."

"Anything else gleaned?"

"He is wealthy, an exaggerator of the truth and, it is whispered, has spoken with Pan."

"Spoken with Pan, my goodness." Woolley sipped his drink, holding up one finger for silence. "Ah."

Clemency punched him on the shoulder. "Darling, you must stop doing that."

Cecil rubbed his shoulder exaggeratedly. "Doing what, darling? I am ignorant of what offends."

"The demanding silence when you sip your martini."

"But darling, that is out of respect for Benedict." Woolley looked at Benedict. "A true artist."

Benedict smiled. "Thank you, sir. My advice to you is avoid him if you can, take what he says with a grain of salt but … " he reached in to his pocket and pulled out a small red silk satchel tied with a thin gold rope, "… carry salt also."

Woolley took the bag.

"Darling?" questioned Clemency.

"Can't be too careful. Our protector Benedict is of the belief that there is more to Mr. Moffatt St. Andrew Woodside-Chang than we can see."

Clemency smiled nervously. "How much more can there be of that enormous man?"

"Quite a lot," said Benedict, "and not all of this physical world. Now sir, if that is all, I will return to my cabin. I've reserved your breakfast for in-cabin and your place for lunch in the dining car. I've taken the liberty and laid out the itinerary for tomorrow. A number of brief yet historically interesting stops."

"Thank you, Benedict," said Woolley, taking the paper. "Ah, mystical yurts!"

"Oh Benedict, if it weren't for Woolley," swooned Clemency.

"Ma'am."

"Steady on, darling."

Benedict left the cabin, closing the door without a sound.

Clemency drank the icy drink and bit into a rusk. "I felt pure malice from that Woodside-Chang character," she said.

"I thought him nothing but a windbag. All show, smoke and mirrors, no substance, facts and dates wrong. He was surely trying to write himself into a history that had already happened. But yes, as Benedict suggested, we will do our best to avoid him," Woolley said, trying to sound relaxed. He tried a pickle and made a face.

"Goodness, pickley."

Clemency smiled then looked seriously at Woolley and said, "Darling, I know love is about trust and the things unsaid, but what matters are you attending to and why did I have to hear about it third-hand and with that horrible man, no less?"

Woolley frowned, "It is a very small deviation on an otherwise delightful itinerary."

"Well, who are these people that you are willing to go back to? And why are we going to Shanghai if it holds such misery?"

"Clem, can I ask you just to trust me? That time was so dark for me." He took the sack of salt and began pouring a line of it in front of the door. "One day I will tell you all, every detail, but may I tell you in my own time? Much of what I do now came from my experiences then. I saw, saw …," Woolley paused, "… things that in my wildest imagination could not believe to be true. Horrible, horrible things."

Clemency reached over and held Woolley tightly. "Oh, my poor bear."

"I will tell you. I'm not keeping secrets, just not ready is all. In Shanghai we are going to be visiting with the daughter of a man with whom I had the honour of serving in the war. Reginald Shaw. Capt. Reg. Shaw. He married one of the most beautiful and intelligent women in Shanghai, Ye Xuan. Their daughter, Daphne, was this charming, patient thing. I must have been quite a sight, the mess that I was, but they stayed with me, the three of them, never giving up and — well darling, here I am."

"Oh darling, you can tell me in your time or not. I

take it Captain Shaw is no longer with us?"

"No, died… killed actually, his wife also. One of the many uprisings. They got in the way. Horrific, the students expelling the communists. Wrong place, wrong time. He was beheaded as a fan kuei, a Foreign Devil." Woolley was angry. "Devil…ha! He was the kindest man alive. And she … I don't want to talk about that just now. Thankfully Daphne survived."

"How horrible!"

"I abhor all violence. It solves nothing. Creates only more violence. I try to never hate, darling, but I do hate violence, brutality and death, however understandable."

"Oh darling, how can beheading an innocent person be understandable?"

"You have to look at the history there. The opium trade was big business, an excellent money spinner for us English; the French too, and the Dutch for that matter. In the 1830s the Chinese Emperor commanded his commissioner to seize all opium from the foreigners and stop us from trading the stuff. This banning caused a rather lucrative and lazy income to disappear and we English were not happy. We sent gunboats to invade Shanghai and its environs and held the natives hostage until the Emperor agreed to sign a treaty that gave many ruling rights to the English, who then opened up the opium trade again. It was devastating to China, but the English didn't care. What was China to them but a civilization of uncouth coolies?" Woolley shook his head in disgust. "A civilization millennia old! Uncouth!? Since then the English, the French, the German and the Dutch have held Shanghai as their own, treating the Chinese as lesser foreigners in their own land.

No wonder there is bitterness. The English certainly have nothing to be proud of in the word EMPIRE. Shameful. Shameful!" Woolley drank down the dregs of his cocktail then cleared his throat. "So, ahem, yes. Daphne. She runs a print shop of sorts, print shop, tea shop, book shop, gallery, tarot, séances on the side, the usual. We've been corresponding for some time. She seems to be accepted by the Chinese there."

"Is that where we're staying?"

"For a bit. I'm not blood but in a way I'm the only family she has. Something shady has taken place that she didn't want to detail through letters. She asked me to come, us to come, and here we are." Woolley gestured to the pulled window binds. "The middle of Siberia, passing through Mongolia. In love, drinking chilled martinis, on an adventure. Exciting, yes?"

"Oh Woolley, I don't know what to think but I wouldn't have it any other way."

"Shall we finish up and call it a night?"

Clemency yawned uncontrollably. "Yes, there has been an awful lot to absorb: shady characters, uprisings, beheadings. I sense from here on in we will need our wits about us."

Woolley kissed Clemency on the head, "Indeed we will. Thank goodness I have you and Benedict. I would be lost otherwise. Absolutely lost."

Chapter 6

Three days passed with little incident. Cecil and Clemency, with Benedict ensuring their comfort, fell in to the gentle circadian rhythm of life on a train and the long voyage. There were breakfasts in the cabins, followed by walks, reading and cards. Lunches. Conversations with the passengers, cocktails in the bar car or in the cabin, a late dinner and a kind of un-wedded honeymoon for the two not young but in love lovebirds. It wasn't until the fourth day at dinner that they bumped into Moffatt St. Andrew Woodside-Chang again, this time with a small man wearing traditional Chinese dress of black silk with golden dragons delicately embroidered on it.

Clemency spotted Woodside-Chang first and tried to steer Woolley to a booth in the back, but he saw them and waved them over. "My friends," he rumbled. "I have been ill. I regret not sending word, I hope you were not worried."

Woolley bit his tongue and said, "You must forgive us Moffatt — may I address you so? — we've been too busy being in love to notice much."

"Ah, love." Woodside-Chang laughed like a loquacious mountain. "You may find it hard to believe but I was in love once. Lust – of course! Yes! But love. I, too, have loved." He paused and inhaled, closing his eyes, lost in his moment. "The quail is excellent tonight."

Clemency burst out laughing. "Sorry, sorry," she said, putting her hand over her mouth. Woolley frowned but inside was almost liquid with love for her. He turned to Woodside-Chang. "May we be introduced to your companion? I fear we have not been."

"Ah, yes," Woodside-Chang rumbled, "this is Mr. Yu Man-yun. He likes to be called Charles by Westerners as he cannot stand his family name being butchered."

The small man beside St. Andrew Woodside-Chang bowed and smiled. "Delighted. Mr. Chang mentioned you were on board and I was most excited to make your acquaintance."

"What do you do, Mr. Yu?" Clemency asked, not wanting to call him Charles.

Mr. Yu bowed again. "In Shanghai, you will see, you will one night be my guest. I am the co-proprietor of a palace of entertainment, The Great World. Not a sing-song girl to be seen. Just class entertainment, no corruption, no vice, no gangsters. Paris of the Orient. Every night unforgettable."

Woolley smiled. "That sounds lovely. Do you have a card, so we may look you up?"

Mr. Yu gave a wide smile, "You are staying with friends in the French Concession, yes?"

Woolley looked perplexed.

"And you are Cecil Herbert Woolley and Miss de la Tour; your man Benedict is in another part of the train. Sorry, I make it my business to know the business of

Shanghai. A great task but I have many working for me. How do you say in the West ? Many ears to the ground. Many eyes in the shadows."

The waiter came just then. "Your usual, Mr. Woolley, Miss de la Tour?"

For the second time in the presence of Moffatt St. Andrew Woodside-Chang, Clemency shivered perceptively with revulsion.

Chapter 7

That night Clemency had the strangest of dreams — a dream so real and yet so preternatural she began to question her own sanity. In it she awoke in her bunk, unsure of the time, but hours after going to bed. She was parched from all the alcohol and needed a glass of water from the carafe sitting on the table by the window. She swung her legs over the bunk side and reached out for the jug and glass. Suddenly she became aware of a presence aside from Woolley's gentle snoring. A thick eerie presence and with it, a deep, wet breathing. As her eyes adjusted to the darkness she made out a huge black shape sitting in the chair across from her. It was wearing a robe that shimmered and glistened in the dark like passing moonlight in a forest, and a large triangular hat with a symbol of gold emblazoned on the front. She was utterly terrified but could do nothing; she could not move nor make a sound to rouse Woolley. The shape made a low laughing sound and stood up. What little light there was focused on its eyes, a man's eyes, so deep set and dark they were horrifying. They focused on Clemency with such menace. In a low resonating voice, the shape began to chant while pointing two fingers from his right hand at Clemency and waving his left, creating eddies of purple mist. She tried to make out the words but couldn't. The mist grew denser and the cabin filled with an odd scent, the smell of rotting forest, corruption and death. She began to cough and covered her nose with the sleeve of her pyjamas. The chanting continued on and on. She felt her feet being touched and looking down saw a coil of rope slowly twisting around them, binding her feet, knotting itself. She tried to wriggle free, but couldn't move, couldn't make a sound; she was either frozen in a horrific dream or frozen in a horrific spell. She was utterly, utterly terrified. The rope grew larger in length and started moving up her body, pulling her, constricting her like a snake. It slithered between her legs, tangled up her thighs and around her waist. It spiralled around her wrists, pulling them behind her, binding her. It rose up, tangling around her upper arms and around her neck. The shape began to laugh. It spoke aloud, "Oh, this is only a taste of my power!" And it laughed once more. Clemency tried to scream but the rope was on her face; it tangled and coiled around her head, into her mouth, down her throat, deep into her ...

She awoke, tangled in the sheets beside Woolley in his bunk, holding him so hard he startled and mumbled, "Darling, can't breathe." She began to cry uncontrollably. He shook himself out of slumber and turned over. "Darling, what is it?"

"Oh Cecil, it was just awful, just awful." But try as she might to remember, the dream had slipped away.

Chapter 8

For the remainder of the voyage Woolley and Clemency
kept to themselves; from Zamyn-Üüd to Datong they fell
into a gently rocked dream-state of cocktails, books and
love-making. The food was generally unexceptional, but
Benedict seemed to have sway with the kitchen staff and
there was always something extravagant or luxurious to
be found on their trays: one night, caviar; one night, as-
paragus in butter sauce. Their cabin was a warm oasis that
they dared not leave. Benedict came and went each evening with clockwork regularity. The sun rose and set. Night
came and went. Clemency fell deeper and deeper in love.
Watching Woolley shave was a religious experience. His
ritual, his wrists, the way his hand held the straight edge,
lost in concentration, wedging himself within the wash-
room closet for stability. Woolley too could not but admire Clemency's perfection. The way she rolled her stock-
ings off, her distracted look as she read a passage from her
book or did a crossword puzzle, saying the answer aloud,
'iguana'.

They saw no more of Moffatt St. Andrew Woodside-
Chang or Mr. Yu, but on the last night an envelope was
slipped under their door containing two passes to The

Great World, Shanghai's '*premiere house of amusement*,' 1 Xizang Road, Shanghai

In the late afternoon the train slowed to approach the Peking station. Gone was the countryside, replaced now with crooked shanty towns, grey modern European-style buildings, and people. Everywhere, people. Soon the station's spires could be seen casting long shadows below. An endless tangle of greasy rail knot work jostled the train hard left and right as they neared and then entered finally the station — on time.

Woolley and Clemency were ready. On their overnight bags Benedict had left the tickets for the connecting train that would take them south to Shanghai. Woolley lit a cigarette and opened their cabin window. The air smelled of diesel, dust, and cooking oil. Clemency came up beside him and slipped her arm around him. "Thank you for a lovely time," she said.

"And it's just begun," said Woolley. "Who know what awaits us out there? China. Bally big place."

It took them both a moment to gain their land legs when descending to the platform. They had become so used to the rocking motion and now that it was gone they stumbled as if exiting an amusement ride. The station was overflowing with humanity. The times had not been good for China and there were so many sleeping bodies in the station, pushed to the sides, covered in rags. Here, and in Shanghai, was where the poor from the provinces came to find a new life, though most ended up not even finding the means to survive. There was no work, there were no riches, many huddled and died there, sometimes found days later. Girls as young as 12 were sold to taxi-dance salons or sing-song girl brothels. Some made it through, but most were sold down to the knocking shops by the sea ports and train stations to slowly die, poor, forgotten and old at the age of 18. Woolley tried to shake off this grim vision; tried to think that the light which warmed the greasy yellow windows of the station and the quays was pleasant and full of hope even though all it illuminated was grease and litter, puddles of spit, and humanity. Everything had a fine dust to it, a fine dust of despair.

"Darling, our train is there," said Woolley pointing to distract Clemency from the scene around her. "Thankfully it's in, so we can just relax until the train leaves. It's another 15 hours to Shanghai, I'm afraid; what a long time it's been."

"It hasn't felt that long," Clemency said, taking his hand. "It's been one of the loveliest times I've ever had. You too, darling?"

Woolley smiled, "Me too, though I am parched and ever so tired. Let's find our cabin and catch a few."

Coolies crowded up to them left and right, desperate to take their cases. "No, no, we're fine. Fine," said Woolley as kindly as he could, taken aback by the desperation in their eyes yet glad that Benedict had most of their baggage already transferred to the new train.

"Oh Woolley, I'd almost forgotten what a horrible place the world really is," cried Clemency.

"Darling, it's not horrible. Sad, yes — unforgiving, difficult, cruel — but there is always hope. I have to believe that." He stopped and kissed her. "There is always you."

"Oh Woolley."

They found their car and entered without incident. There were very few people on the train just yet. The cleaning staff were still working their way along the dark corridors, dragging huge bags of linen and debris. The cars smelled of cigarette smoke and sweat. Thankfully their cabin, when they found it, had been made up. Woolley slid the glass door back and invited Clemency inside. She huffed onto the bunk as he pulled the curtains on the door and stowed the bags.

There was an envelope on the table under the window addressed to Woolley. He ripped it open.

"Is it from Benedict?" asked Clemency as she reclined.

"No. Not Benedict. This seems to be some sort of … well, I can't really make it out. It looks like a photograph of Daphne's tea shop." He turned it over; nothing was written on the back. He glanced into the envelope again, maybe he had missed something. No, nothing else. "Well, this is interesting. A photo of where we're going. Is it a warning? A …? "

"Could it be a calling card, that Daphne knows we're on the train?"

"Seems rather vague; she would have written something." He handed the card to Clemency. She went pale and immediately dropped it, as if it was hot to the touch.

"What darling, what?" shouted Woolley.

"I swear, I saw … I swear I saw eyes in the card, staring at me."

Woolley looked at the photo carefully. "It's just a picture of a tea shop. Could you have imagined it? We have just spent a fortnight on a train."

"Yes, you're probably right," said Clemency shakily.

Woolley reached down and picked up the card, carefully putting it back in the envelope. A sense of unease overcame him and, as if in sympathy, above the city an enormous storm broke and with it horrendous, humid sheet lightening and deafening thunder.

"Never a dull moment with Cecil Herbert Woolley," said Clemency, regaining her composure and laughing.

"No," said Woolley, "Never."

A few hours later there was a quick rap on the glass of their door. Woolley raised his eyebrow. "Too early for Benedict," and slid it open.

Standing in the aisle was a young porter in a crisp Jinpu Railway uniform. He bowed.

"Mr. Woolley, missive for you."

"Ah, a missive." Woolley reached into his pocket and found he only had rubles. "Oh, I am sorry."

"Not needed," bowed the porter. "A pleasure, sir." And snapping his heels, he slid the cabin door shut.

Woolley turned to Clemency. "We are popular today."

"Now that must be from Benedict."

"Here's hoping," Woolley tore open the envelope.

"Sir,

Forgive me for not preparing your cabin proper-
ly. I had not the opportunity. I hope you find it well
and comfortable. I am forward three cars and will
meet you in Shanghai.

I have sensed a strange presence on this train
which I would like to advise you and Miss de la
Tour to be aware of. It does not seem to have form,

it is just a feeling, an ill wind. I do not like it and
advise caution at all times.
    I remain, most faithful.
    Benedict."

Woolley frowned and passed the note to Clemency. "An ill wind," mused Clemency. "I am worried, Cecil. Are you sure we should be embarking on this adventure?"

Woolley smiled and lit two cigarettes, passing one to Clemency. "You will like Daphne, and Shanghai is marvellous. When the light hits it a certain way... Lots to see and do. It will be lovely darling, just lovely." Clemency looked into Woolley's eyes, knowing full well that he believed what he was saying about as much as she did.

Chapter 9

Benedict had thoughtfully arranged for dinner and drinks in their compartment. After, they found themselves exhausted and soon fell fast asleep, hardly noticing as the train slipped out of the station. The track ran through a busy city street making progress slow, the engineer repeatedly blowing his horn for people to move their chickens and goats out of the way.

Once the train cleared the city, it quickened pace and sped off with confidence towards the south and Shanghai. The route kept inland and reasonably straight, passing through rolling countryside and now and then a city until it finally banked west at Nanjing, before heading towards the river.

It was early afternoon when they finally stepped onto the Shanghai station platform. They were again greeted with the smell of grease and humanity. The air was hot and wet, making it difficult to breath, and it left an odd taste as it went in the mouth. The open rafters of the roof pierced the tracks with shafts of hard white light.

"Good Lord," said Woolley, breaking instantly into a sweat. "Forgot about the heat."

"This is unholy; I will be a moist sight to behold when we do meet Daphne," Clemency said, fanning herself with her hat. Woolley pulled down their overnight luggage; he was grateful they had packed sparingly. The platform was jammed with people of every nation, dressed in everything from the latest haute monde to beggars' rags.

A skeletal man in a broken felt hat came up to them and shouted, "Catchee one piece rickshaw? B'long my pidgin. Catchee chop chop!"

"Good lord," replied Woolley.

Clemency stepped forward and in Mandarin asked if the gentleman would help with the bags and find them a rickshaw. She then handed him some coins. The man, obviously taken aback, scooped up their luggage and said, "This way."

Cecil lit a cigarette. "You speak Mandarin?"

"Father taught me."

"Ah."

The man, carrying the luggage under his arms, navigated the crowd expertly with Clemency and Woolley following hard at his heels. The crowd was even denser within the huge stone station, the sound of humanity echoing frantically. The man darted out the front doors and Clemency and Woolley went with him. The blinding light and the intense heat hit them like a slap in the face. Woolley instantly felt perspiration run down the centre of his back and into his shorts.

"Good lord," he said, putting his hand up to shade his eyes.

"I fear I've lost track of our man," Clemency said with only a slight hint of panic.

"That's him there, isn't it?" asked Woolley, pointing at a man rushing towards them pulling a rickshaw. "Don't suppose I could get a drink before this journey; I sense it will be a challenging one."

"Darling, let's just get to where we are going. I'm dying for a bath."

"Bath, yes. Sensible of you, sensible."

The thin man with the rickshaw pulled up in front and gestured for them to get in. They were fortunate to luck onto a reasonably clean conveyance, with only a few chicken feathers, puddles of spit and a canopy to shade them. Their luggage was strapped on the front beside their feet.

"Do you know where we are going?" Clemency asked.

"Oh, right, that would help." Woolley rummaged in his jacket pocket and brought out a letter. "The address is on the top. It's in the French Concession." Clemency took the paper and read the address aloud to the man. "Chop chop" he said, and they jostled off.

"I find this embarrassing," Woolley said, turning to Clemency. "You know the word 'coolie' is thought to be Urdu or quite possibly from the Turkish word for slave. I just find it upsetting. Here more than anywhere, I am not proud of my Englishness."

"Darling, live by example, that is just where you are from, not who you are."

"Good lord, Clemency, as an Englishmen that kind of talk is akin to treason."

Clemency smiled and put a handkerchief to her face to mask the foul air and dust.

The rickshaw driver took a snaking route covering more of the city than expected. Woolley was amused but said nothing, thinking Clemency would enjoy this small tour. They were taken down to the waterfront, the Bund with its striking yet incongruous mixture of European building styles: Paris, Berlin and the Riviera all muddled and whitewashed with a thick coat of yearning, covered in soot, and filled with corrupt and spent expats who could never return to the homeland they so vehemently identified with. Woolley knew greed had paved these streets and the wide promenades. Greed had pushed the Chinese away from the port, and yet had left it remarkably underdeveloped. Beside enormous cargo ships, dilapidated junks still sat tied to moor posts greasy with the ooze of the Huangpu River and the East China Sea.

They passed by the Cathay Hotel. "Tiffin at the Peking Room," mumbled Woolley.

"What darling?"

"Tiffin, that's what lunch is called at the Cathay."

"Oh, thank you darling."

Woolley pointed to a forlorn building on the jetty with a rather large clock mounted in it. "They call that Big Ching."

Clemency held Woolley's arm and took it all in. She had travelled extensively, but never to the East. This was sensory overload. Cars swerved at them, men and children shouted, animals were tied to truck beds, things were being bought and sold all around them, the high and the low. It was all here. Woolley smiled and kissed Clemency's head. "It is quite something, isn't it? When the sun goes down and the lights come out Shanghai becomes another city, it's the city of blazing light."

"Oh Woolley," said Clemency, and kissed him on the lips.

Eventually the driver snaked his rickshaw into a quieter and much more lush section of the city. Passing a few pocked and sad walls, the signs all changed to French and the trees seemed to stand loftier, yet still had a forlorn air as if beaten by the sunlight and heat. Daphne's bookshop was off the Rue de Consulat, a labyrinth of streets still lined with original Chinese shops and permanently darkened alleys that gradually opened to more shops and marvellous wonders. It felt cooler here, sleepier. A rickshaw leisurely passed them containing an elegant woman in a tight-fitting green shift, fanning herself. She looked at Woolley and Clemency with disdain. "A secondary wife returning," said Woolley.

"What?"

"The term for afternoon dalliances."

"Oh Woolley, the things you know."

They pulled up to a narrow pedestrian alley o'er hung with streamers and red lanterns. The driver shouted to Clemency, who turned to Woolley. "It is down there, but he can't go any further."

"I can't really remember the shop. When I was here, we stayed in the International Concession. Much of that time is lost to me, but if your chum says this is the place, I am willing to take his word for it."

Clemency squeezed his hand before they dismounted, feeling more than a little disorientated and more than a little sore. Woolley took the bags off the cart while Clemency haggled over the price. "Darling, I'm trying to make him take more than he's charging, but he won't."

"It's not worth the risk," Woolley offered. "He and the rickshaw are owned by the local thugs; each day he must give up all the money he earns and then he is paid a small fee. If they find money unaccounted for, they will beat him senseless."

The thin man took his fee and trundled off looking exhausted and drained.

"Woolley," said Clemency.

"Yes dear."

"What is this place?"

"Why it's the Paris of the East, the Whore of Asia, Heaven and Hell all bundled up in one very dangerous package. Shropshire off-season, but only more so," he grinned. "Shall we begin?" And picking up the luggage, he offered her his arm and they entered the darkened passage.

Chapter 10

As they stepped into the alley the city sounds stopped. The air ceased to move, and the filtered light took on a preternatural glow as if lit through gauze. The alley opened into drowsy corridor of small shops and tiny cafés. Now and then a food stall. It was now late afternoon and with the heat, everyone was doing as little as possible. The shops were all black wood, ornate like beautiful haunted boxes, their windows gleaming and clean, the light inside ochre. The colour red was everywhere; in lanterns hung in front of shops and hanging above, in the flags and banners, in the dresses and the light. Clemency asked a vendor the address and he pointed across what could be called a square, save that it was a rectangle. "He says there, that alley by the herb shop."

Woolley picked up the bags and made a noise; the heat was making all things difficult. As they crossed over to the shop, various children ran up to Clemency and touched her.

"Oh dear, that does make me uncomfortable."

"They, like me, think of you as a goddess," said Woolley

"Oh dear."

Woolley noticed something unsettling about the herb shop as they approached. Their wares seemed more esoteric than medicinal, there were strange weights and levels on display, symbols, charts and even a pentagram. Nasty stuff, he thought, and as if to cement the unpleasantness, out of the shop door waddled Moffatt St. Andrew Woodside-Chang.

Woolley winced and nudged Clemency, who upon seeing him, blanched.

"Why, Mr. Woolley and Miss de la Tour." Woodside-Chang oozed, folding the black sack he had in his huge hands and pushing it into the pocket of his soiled white linen jacket. "What an absolute pleasure and what an auspicious coincidence if, I should add, one believed in coincidence."

"Indeed," replied Woolley, so tired and disorientated he was unable to hide his annoyance. "We just arrived, just pulled into town. Remarkable you 're here already."

"Yes, well, this is my part of the world, so to speak, and I know my way. But you must be exhausted from your journey. May I buy you some tea? There is an excellent shop around here," he said, looking straight at Woolley.

"Terribly kind, terribly kind of you but we are dusty and in need of stillness and, I suspect, a bath."

"Ah well, I will walk with you to make sure of your safe arrival."

Woolley gritted his teeth and caught Clemency's eye. Neither wanted this man in their lives and Woolley especially did not want Woodside-Chang to know their final destination.

"No, no," said Woolley, "we couldn't trouble you."

But Woodside-Chang had already charged off down the alley, his huge girth sucking up all the air. Woolley picked up the bags and followed. Clemency was hesitant but realizing she had no choice, joined him.

The alley was much smaller than the previous ones, the space barely wide enough for two people side-by-side or one fat St. Andrew Woodside-Chang. It opened onto a narrow street where all the shops were of the same black wood, many with gaily decorated displays. Woolley noticed they were mostly map, book and curio shops. One establishment sold brass instruments, another nautical curiosities. The signs were a jumble of Chinese characters mixed with French and English.

As he kept walking, Woodside-Chang turned back and bellowed, "On your right is the tea shop I was suggesting. It is good to take note, establishments such as this are rare."

Clemency, exhausted and overcome by the heat, blurted out, "Wait please! Wait, this is it, No. 8."

"Ha!" bellowed Woodside-Chang as he turned back. "Dare I comment?!"

Clemency realized what she had done and almost started to cry.

Woolley, seeing this, reached out his hand to Woodside-Chang. "Well, thank you Moffatt, thank you so much. We will take it from here. It's been a long journey. Once we've settled we can all get together and have a lovely chat. For now, we are so exhausted, and I would very much like to meet my friend unencumbered, shall we say."

St. Andrew Woodside-Chang was visibly angry but

backed off and pulled something out of his pocket.

"My card," he said, a slow, creeping smile curling upon his face. "Do please keep in touch. I shall hunt you out if I do not hear from you within the fortnight. Remember, Mr. Yu promised a night on the town and I for one would like to take advantage of that." Turning suddenly, he grabbed Clemency's hand and kissed it. "Charmed." He then shook Woolley's hand violently and bounded off down the alley.

They watched him until he was gone. Clemency visibly shook with revulsion. "I do not like that man."

"No darling, nor do I. Nor do I like that he just 'happened' to be in the area. I do not like it one bit." He paused. "But deep breath, we have Daphne to meet."

Woolley turned to face a lovely and quaint establishment, which like all the others had an exterior of black wood and small pane windows. He reached for the door and gestured to Clemency to follow. Clemency did not move.

"Cecil, beside you, on both sides!" she whispered urgently.

Woolley looked but there was nothing except the two stalls with books and the passing crowd. "I see nothing, darling."

Clemency started to point to them, but they were gone.

"You didn't see them? There were two."

"Two what, darling? Two what? Honestly you are tired, the heat, let's just get inside…"

"Oh Woolley, I do not like it here." She lurched towards Cecil and wrapped her arms around him just as the shop door flung open and a man dressed entirely in black flew past them shouting, "It's in the cards, he is there! Your fate depends on your listening, obeying. The spirits do not lie, young lady! Your reward for mocking them will be dreadful and black!"

"Good lord," said Woolley, and with Clemency in his arms opened the door.

A bell tinkled as they entered the shop. Inside, it was quiet and still. The walls were a lovely, worn ochre, the tables and booths done in black leather. To one side the wall was lined with an enormous ebony bookcase that ran from floor to tin-covered ceiling. On the other side there sat a bar with a huge shining espresso machine and a wall of red lacquer boxes, tea pots and cups. All around there were hundreds of pictures of people and places, letters and beautiful banners of Chinese calligraphy. Above, a ceiling fan slowly turned, rippling a piece of red tissue that was hung over a brass Buddha that sat above the bar. Seated at a small round table near the bar was a girl, her head in her hands, her shoulders convulsing as she silently sobbed.

Woolley cleared his throat. "Daphne?"

She looked up and focused, then jumped up and threw her arms around Cecil. "Oh, Mr. Woolley."

"Oh, my dear girl, oh my dear girl, what is happening here? What just happened? Who was that man?"

Daphne burst back into tears. Cecil held her until she quieted. Clemency stood by awkwardly, then moved and touched Cecil on the arm. "I will get a glass of water."

Daphne pulled back, wiping her eyes as she pushed the hair away from her face, "Oh I am so sorry, I am so … you must be Clemency, I am so thrilled to meet you." She held out a thin, pale hand.

Clemency took her hand, "Can I get you some water?"

"No, no, yes actually, yes, I feel awful."

She was so tiny, barely there, her hair thick and black, her eyes sunken and dark. Woolley let her go. Stepping back, he thought she was quite possibly the second most beautiful creature in the entire world.

Chapter 11

"Now, from the beginning," said Woolley, locking the door. "Who was that man, and what was he shouting about?"

Daphne sipped her water. Clemency, sitting beside Woolley, looked at the girl with concern.

"He is a mun mai poh, what you call a psychic. Mr. Bannington-Smythe. He said he knew Father, that Father … oh Mr. Woolley …"

"Please, I am Cecil, and this is Clemency. We are family."

She blew her nose on a napkin. "He said he knew father, that father was speaking to him…"

"Speaking to him? What, before his death?"

"No Mr. Wooll … Cecil. Now. From beyond the grave … oh it's too terrible. Father never mentioned this man. Why would he … What does he want …?"

Cecil placed his hand on her arm; she was trembling. "Did he say what your f ather wanted?"

Daphne looked up with her huge black eyes. "You don't believe him, do you?!"

"I didn't say that, I am just trying to understand."

"I am so worried, Mr. Woolley."

"Cecil."

"Cecil."

"And Clemency."

Daphne again blew her nose. "I am so worried, I am doing my best to keep the shop running. When Mother and Father were killed I gave them the best ceremony I could; I knew their ghosts would be troubled after how they died … oh it was so horrible. I burned money and paper books for Father to read, and clothes and food. I did my best. But Mr. Bannington-Smythe is telling me that Father and Mother are wandering and lost, they cannot afford to pass over, that I didn't burn enough. I don't know what to do. Oh, I don't know what to do … ."

Cecil looked at Clemency, who was looking at Daphne with utter concern. Clemency leaned forward and gave Daphne a fresh hanky. "Darling, Cecil and I will get to the bottom of this. We are here now; as Cecil said, we are family. Can you close the shop for a few days, so you can rest? I think what you need most is sleep and food and love."

"Oh, I daren't close. He'll know, they'll know something is wrong."

"Who will know," asked Woolley. "Who?"

Suddenly a huge shadow walked by the window and there came a loud rapping. Daphne tensed and Woolley put his hands to his lips to indicate silence. The rapping continued and a voice boomed out, "Come, come now Mr. Woolley, I know you are there." Woolley sighed and got up to unlock the door.

There, blocking what little light there was, stood Moffatt St. Andrew Woodside-Chang.

Woolley was indignant, "Good Lord man, didn't we

just..." Woodside-Chang raised his hand to shush him. "Sir, I came to apologize. After leaving I realized my rudeness in forcing myself upon you, thinking, as only a Hermit and student of solitude can, that you and Miss de la Tour were in need of guidance. I merely wanted to show you my Shanghai, not interfere in family matters. I came to offer you my apologies and to say should you ever need assistance in anything, no matter how trivial, I am available."

Woolley was not moved, nor did he believe that this was an innocent offer of assistance. "Well, yes, thank you,' he said curtly. Looking back at Clemency and Daphne, he saw that both were staring at Woodside-Chang with dread, but the man seemed oblivious. Woolley was about to abandon his usual tactfulness and was considering shoving him out the door.

"Mr. Woolley, something I quite forgot to give you. You see, I am a humble poet, a scribbler. I had hoped to give this to you on the train, but alas we seemed to miss each other. Please would you be so kind as to accept my gift of Volume One of my collected poems. I had it privately printed in Barcelona in '05, goodness so long ago." He handed Woolley a slim volume bound in black calf's leather with gold embossing and marbled edges. Woolley thought, does he carry these with him? He also had no desire to take or touch anything from Woodside-Chang, but he was an Englishman first and the only thing lower than being impolite was a confrontation. He took the book. "Thank you, Moffatt. Most kind," he said as he gestured to the door.

"Please, let me inscribe it. It does not increase the

value, but it does give me pleasure in knowing my words are in your collection. Now, ah ..." he patted himself, "my pen."

Frustrated, Woolley reached into his pocket and drew out his fountain-pen. Woodside-Change, impressed, took a moment to inspect it. It seemed a tiny thing in the man's huge hands. "What a marvelous pen."

"A gift."

"Ah, an admirer?"

"No," Woolley replied, looking straight at Clemency.

Woodside-Chang smiled indulgently. "I do so marvel at love. The heart is such a weak and leaky vessel and yet we are forever setting adrift in it." He absently scribbled his signature into the book, then capping the pen and giving it the once-over again handed it back to Woolley, who took it as if it had been soiled. "Now, I shall trouble you no longer today, for family time is precious time." He stared across the room directly at Daphne. "And I see your young friend has a lifetime of sorrows ahead of her, so I am sure she is in need ... of family. "

"Well, yes, quite," said Woolley, reaching for the door.

"Until we meet again," said Woodside-Chang, taking Woolley's hand and shaking it. Looking directly at Clemency, he added, "And I look forward to our next time, Miss de la Tour," and then to Daphne, "and to getting to know you better Miss Shaw." He made an odd little bow and with the clang of the door bell he was gone, leaving only an odd energy and a cloud of scent.

"G'lord," breathed out Woolley, the relief written over his face. "I was expecting a puff of smoke or a thunderclap. I do not know that man, but I would not trust him with my pen, let alone my life."

Daphne ran forward and hugged Woolley. "Oh Cecil, that is what's been happening for months. Strange people coming in, acting as if they know me, or want to get to know me, telling me about things as if they are inevitable, as just about to happen. They say prophesied over and over. They tell me that Father and Mother are in trouble. That Mother is cross, that I must sell the shop, that I must go to a monastery. I am beside myself. It is still very painful and now these people are stirring it up, bringing it all back. What do they want? What do they want from me?"

Clemency took Daphne in her arms and held her. She gave a pleading look to Woolley who went over and poured another glass of water for the girl.

"Strange things are in play here," said Woolley after a long silence. "Woodside-Chang was not a coincidence. I fear there is some elaborate and evil game being played and we are caught in the middle."

Woolley let Daphne settle. He watched as Clemency took charge. Here was a person who had just spent the last eight days on a train, ridden hours in a rickshaw, met unpleasant after unpleasant people ... And yet here she was, tenderly holding a girl she'd never met, never knew existed until a few days ago, filled to the brim with compassion and love; she was calmness collected and, quite frankly, simply the most beautiful thing on the planet Earth.

"Daphne, we are here to help you, to find out what's happening." Woolley began pacing. "The traditions of this country are deep-rooted and fraught with belief, omen and superstition. They are as ancient as the hills." Woolley touched an octagonal Fung Shui mirror hung near the door, "but I will do my best to – respectfully – unweave this nasty sweater you are tangled up in."

"Woolley, your metaphors!" laughed Clemency.

"A sticky web! A pilling sweater!" chortled Woolley.

"Thank you, Cecil," Daphne said quietly, pushing her hair back behind her ears. "I am so glad you are here." She stood up and bowed deeply, "May I formally welcome you to my unworthy house." Wooley and Clemency awkwardly returned the bow.

"You must both be exhausted and dusty. A trunk arrived for you this afternoon and I had them place it in your room. What an unworthy host I have been. I am so sorry to start your arrival with such drama."

"Daphne, please!" Clemency began, "There is nothing to worry about, we are here, in one piece, or two pieces actually…"

"Three darling, as Benedict must be somewhere!"

"Then three pieces, but we are really all one, one family."

Woolley cleared his throat. "I don't suppose I could get a restorative drink?"

"Woolley!" shot back Clemency. "Time and place!"

"Exactly darling, here and now. I am as parched as a cactus plant in Ciudad Juárez during the dry season!"

"Oh Cecil," grinned Daphne, her mood lightening slightly. "You came all this way for me. At least I can properly feed you and Father did teach me all manner of Western drinks. His bar is upstairs in the library."

Woolley felt loved.

Daphne led them to the back of the room. There was

a red curtain with a delicate floral pattern in gold embroidery, which she pulled back to reveal a wooden panel. She pressed three fingers into knot holes, holding them until there was a faint click. With that she slid the panel aside to reveal a stairwell leading up to the above floors. A cool scent of incense and wood wafted down from above.

Clemency brushed down her travelling pants and took Daphne's hand. "Daphne, I know we are going to be great friends. Woolley already knows you, so he has me at a disadvantage."

"As a child!" said Woolley.

"Oh Clemency, he knew me when I was ten. I hope I've changed some."

"You still have that sparkle I remember," smiled Woolley. "You've grown into the picture of the best parts of both your parents. I know they would be so proud of you."

Daphne burst out in tears again. Woolley frowned. Clemency breathed in deep and once again took Daphne in her arms. "Poor girl," she whispered to Woolley, "she's at her end."

She gave Daphne a hug. "You simply must let me help with dinner but first I must bathe and change, as I feel as if I've lived three life times in these clothes."

Daphne smiled, and taking Clemency's hand guided her up the carpeted stairs.

Woolley went back to check on the lock. With the light fading, this strange little shop became a twilight-filled oasis. Outside shadows showed the evening bustle as people went about their business as the heat subsided. Inside, cooled by the quiet and the wood, there was stillness. Woolley breathed in the scents of polish and incense, of teas and soap; he breathed in the tranquility. For nearly a fortnight he and Clemency had had nothing but noise: the trains and cars, the shouting of humans and the discord of life in the city. For the first time in what felt like such a long time, the world wasn't rushing past under his feet, and he was enveloped in glorious, almost liquid silence. He pulled the shop blinds down and shot the extra bolt in the door. No one would come in tonight if he could help it. But could he ?

Chapter 12

Woolley considered his options. All the bottles were covered
in a light layer of dust. There were gins he had not heard
of in queer-shaped bottles (tempting), and strangely coloured glass (upsetting). He knew the word gin in many
languages but there were some here that were a complete
mystery to him. He decided on three bottles with dark
labels written in Hanzi. He opened the first and sniffed
– a delicious swirl of juniper, gin. Hm. And something
else, ginger perhaps? The next smelled of tangerine. The
third of jasmine. Delicious. Delicious. He decided on the
jasmine. Behind him was a small ice box and what looked
like mango sorbet. Inside the box was a delicate porcelain
bowl filled with irregularly-shaped chipped ice. He took
it out and placed it on the counter. Shaker. Ah, lovely.
Now ... tongs. Behind him was a black lacquer shelving
unit, inlaid with mother of pearl cranes and ivory flowers.
Woolley paused to admire its delicate perfection. On top,
in a blue and white ink brush jar, sat a number of lovely
bar instruments: strainer, sieve, and yes, ice tongs. Bless
you, Captain Reginald Shaw, you taught your daughter
well. Reggie. Old chap. Old friend. The tongs were shaped
like dragon's claws. He removed them from the vessel and

with them chose three pleasingly-shaped chips of ice. In the shaker, he swirled a drop of vermouth and then dumped it into another porcelain bowl with more cranes and flowers. He then took the scented gin and …

"Woolley!"

"Eh! Oi!"

Clemency made a face. "You haven't been paying attention at all."

"Of course, I have, my darling. I've decided to try the jasmine. Never had … "

"Woolley, for the past quarter of an hour Daphne and I have been talking to you. Where have you been?"

"I've been right here, darling, all the time. Right here. In the moment. Forgive me Daphne, we spoke of drinks and it became a focus. I wasn't aware that the meeting had begun without me. Just let me shake, pour and I am all yours 120%." He smiled. "Anyone joining me?"

"I, Woolley," said Clemency, "would just like some water."

"Or tea?" added Daphne. "We have so much lovely tea … being a tea shop. Some Pu-erh perhaps, which will restore your vitality lost by travel."

"That sounds lovely, Daphne. Woolley, would you like your vitality restored?"

"Sounds like reliving my teens. No, I will stick to my own vice of gin," he chuckled and began to shake the shaker vigorously.

Daphne went downstairs and came back with a lovely dark-red lacquer box decorated with bats — the symbol for happiness — and a blue and white porcelain tea pot, also decorated with bats. She opened a drawer in the large mahogany desk that sat to one side and took out a small black cast-iron kettle and what looked like a small ornate turtle. Placing the items on the table in front of Clemency, she struck a match, lit the back of the turtle and placed the small pot on top. Clemency watched as Daphne concentrated, much like Woolley, on the minutia of the preparation. The aromatic leaves were scooped out of the small box with a small silver spoon and placed into tea pot.

"Goodness! That is pungent," Clemency said. "I cannot place the smell. It's not one I would say has a totally pleasant scent."

"It smells like a remembered barnyard," Daphne said. Woolley, hearing this over the shaking, raised an eyebrow. Daphne poured the now boiling water into the pot and flipped a small hourglass in the shape of a Daoist monk. "Pu-erh is a very ancient tea. It was originally produced for those living in the more remote areas of China. To transport it easily, merchants compressed it into slabs and bricks but exposure to moisture in the warehouses and on the long journeys resulted in a fungal fermentation that… "

"Ah, Daphne," said Clemency, "maybe best we let the tea speak for itself."

"Oh, I do apologize, I was being a tea shop girl. I just find it fascinating. Like cheese. It's really just rotted milk or gin, which is just… "

"Stop now, Daphne," joked Woolley, and pouring out his drink and raising a hand for silence, he sipped. "Ah. How simply delicious."

The sand in the hourglass ran through. Daphne took

up the pot and poured out two small cups of the steaming brew. Both women picked up the small cups and sipped.

"Oh!" exclaimed Clemency, "I wasn't expecting that. Delicious."

Woolley frowned, but feeling now revived from his martini he turned to Daphne. "Now, we are here, we are restored, and we are at your service."

"Oh, Cecil, that sounds so bad, you are my guests …"

"Daphne, there is nothing I desire more than to be at your service, believe me. The daughter of my great friend and former protector… it is an absolute, absolute honour." He clouded briefly as unbidden dark memories came to the fore, then continued. "Now, from the beginning, what is going on? Why your letter? Who are these men prophesying about you?"

"And," interjected Clemency, "What is the meaning of those two figures by the front door?"

Daphne grew pale. "Figures by the door? Oh god," she put her hands to her mouth, "you can see them also?! They're spirits. Ghosts," she cried. "If you can see them, Clemency, then they must real. Ox and Goat."

Woolley then knew what she was referring to, what Clemency had seen. Guards were here. The *niu tou ma mian*. What is going on, he thought to himself and began to feel ill at ease. He walked over to Daphne and sat down and wrapped his arms around her. "As I said, we are here, you are safe now. We will get to the bottom of this."

Daphne burst into tears. Woolley frowned and pulled out a clean handkerchief, daubing at her eyes. "Now Daphne, let's try again. Why don't we start at the beginning, ah, well, not the beginning beginning, but when all this started happening? When it got to the point where you felt my assistance was needed? "

Daphne closed her eyes. She couldn't stop the tears. She sighed slightly while collecting her thoughts. "I have been doing my best to keep the shop going, to keep myself going since my parents were … died. Father kept meticulous records, so it wasn't that hard to sit down and take over. Also, I lived a large part of my life in this shop. It is my home. As you know, mother's family essentially disowned us; they were so unhappy with the match. We became an island of three, plus the circle of eccentric friends that became our extended family. And I'm sure you know the sort of friends we had." She smiled, then said wistfully, "The friends I had." She wrapped her hands around the bowl of tea. "But no one ever got too close as Father chose his friends very carefully; so many were still slightly suspicious of him. Society treated him, us really, as if we were just visitors though we lived here, and Father spoke the language … languages. Mother was from here, but the English world is so bigoted and petty, they would not let her into their society. And they shunned Father for much the same reason they shunned Mother. They had crossed … the line. Chinese society was much the same, so we made do with our own society. Mother had a gift and was conducting séances, which were becoming increasingly popular as everyone in Shanghai has lost someone dear to them, that they need to urgently speak with. There was card reading, tea leaves. Free thinkers and poets came here. Father ran the tea shop and book store like an oasis to the disenfranchised, which, aside from the moneyed class, was basically everyone here.

One morning an Englishman came into the shop saying he knew Father from his war years. He acted like he was an old chum. I was there and could tell Father had no idea or memory of who this person was, but for politeness played along. The man said he flew in the same squadron, spoke of similar friends, and he even knew you, Cecil. Father was very uncomfortable, and Mother was not impressed as when he spoke, he also seemed to be taking stock of the store, its contents, as if looking for something. He knew of Mother's abilities and spoke of them with reverence but in the condescending way white people use here with the Chinese. He said he was only in town for a couple of days and wanted to take us to Tiffin. He bid farewell, saying he wanted to explore the city on his own and would return later. But in a way it felt like he had not left. His presence was so great, even his cologne lingered long after he had gone. And at 4:45 bell on the front door rang and the man walked in. He was dressed more formally, in an evening coat and a derby hat; very inappropriate for the heat. He had a small flat black bag with him. He was carrying flowers, which he gave to my mother and a beautiful hand-bound journal, which he gave to me.

He then smiled, and I remember being afraid of that smile, and he reached into his black bag and pulled out a deck of cards with a red dragon on the back and gave them to Father.

Woolley interrupted, "Playing cards?"

"Yes."

"Tarot?"

"No, nothing like I had ever seen. Not Western cards,

not any gaming cards Chinese use. These had symbols and shapes, triangles on them. And circles. I thought for a moment he had given Father some sort of fantastic flash card game, like the ones we had in school. I remember Father was taken aback; he looked at the cards, still in the stranger's hands and said, ' Are those…?"

'Yes,' said the man, 'the *Egui* deck. A reproduction I am sure, but even a reproduction is rarer than the rarest of rubies.'

'But those decks change hands at 1,000 yen,' gasped Mother.

'More now actually, what with conflicts ahead, but I got them for next to nothing, for a song.'

'I simply couldn't accept these as a gift,' father shuddered uncomfortably.

'Sir,' the man straightened, 'You more than once saved my life and for that I owe you my own.'

"How?" asked Woolley, "Was your father beginning to remember who this was? Saved his life? I remember none of this."

"Father thought and thought. Suddenly the man went very pale and almost fainted. My mother guided him to a table and gave him a glass of water. He seemed revived but when he stood up, he almost fainted again. Tiffin was forgotten and we settled the stranger into the guest room. He would accept no food, just a bowl of tea. He seemed to be grateful that Father asked him to stay; Father couldn't lose face and not ask. It was so strange for me at the time. My parents were always a rock to me, so steady, but that night they were visibly shaken by this man.

'He can only stay one night,' Father said in a firm

whisper. 'There is a debt, but I don't know what it is.'

We had a quiet evening. It was our custom to read but none could concentrate with that man in the house. In China, a stranger is a warning, like a crow, a messenger, a sign. My parents both feared what this message could be. Eventually we all went to bed. I continued to try and read by lamplight, but I could hear my parents talking agitatedly in their room. When I fell asleep I dreamed of a tunnel. I can't remember the specifics, but I do remember to this day the smell of the earth, freshly dug, and a glow, a green glow. It was early morning when I awoke. My parents always rose early as there was always something to be done before the shop could open. When I joined them for breakfast, Mother looked so drawn and Father was ashen and had not shaved. I will never forget how frightened he looked.

We drank tea and ate rice, listening for the stranger to wake, hoping secretly he had left in the night. Eventually Father could wait no longer as he had to open the shop. He pushed himself up from the table. Mother threw him a worried glance. She reached out and took my hand as Father mounted the stairs and went to the guest room. Eventually he came down, alone, carrying the stranger's bag.

'He is gone,' said Father, sounding slightly relieved. 'All he left was this. The bed had not been slept in, there was nothing, no sign of him ever existing, just this bag.'

Mother took it from him and rifled through it, I think hoping to find an explanation, something, a name. She pulled out ball after ball of wadded newspaper. They smelled awful, so pungent, of dust and mold. Mother became frantic; the balls of paper seemed to have no end. She dropped them all over the floor. Father put his hand on her arm worriedly. She then pulled out a small tin — a ration tin from the war that usually contained chocolates or cigarettes. Mother held it up for Father, who took it from her cautiously.

'Careful,' she said.

He opened it. Inside was a clipping from a French newspaper: a war notice. So small it could be missed. 'English Plane Bombs Orchard. Kills 17 Children.'

'What does it mean?' Mother asked.

Father sat down as though the wind had been taken out of him; minutes later he spoke. 'We were testing a new plane. Myself, Woolley and a man named Carmichael. It had never been tried before successfully — an aircraft carrying so many bombs. I couldn't distance it enough in my head, which is what I had to do to not go mad. This machine will hasten the end of the war, they said. But how? By killing in greater quantities more quickly? It was madness. But by then I couldn't believe there was any-one left to kill. The fields in France were knee deep in the dead. Woolley flew, Carmichael was gunner and I navi-gated and operated the bomb bay. We were just testing it, seeing if the plane could hold the weight. We took off awkwardly; Woolley wasn't used to it. It was a lovely day. I remember that so clearly. Unlimited ceiling. Gorgeous blue. Then suddenly something went wrong. The rudder was not responding. We couldn't manoeuvre. We listed, our weight too great. Something then snapped, a wire, it tangled in the exposed mechanics. We were going down. I panicked. 'Woolley,' I shouted, 'We have to let go of the cargo.' He didn't hear; or wouldn't hear as we knew it would mean the bombs. 'Woolley!' We were descending at an incredible speed. I put my hand on the bomb lever and I remember Carmichael leaving the gunner bay and coming towards me. He was pointing down and shouting something I couldn't hear over the engines. Then another wire broke, hitting Carmichael and releasing the bombs from the bomb rack. 16 bombs and one man fell out of the listing plane that day and into the air. The plane lurched back up. I looked below and saw an old manor house and an orchard in full bloom — a gorgeous patch of pink that had not be beaten down by mans' ugliness. Schoolchildren were playing, I could see them running, just tiny specks really, but towards the orchard. I couldn't look away as the bombs hit, and the explosions turned the pink to red to … black … to nothing … Horrible, just horrible.' We sat in silence as Father wept into his hands.

'But Father,' I said, 'What does that have to do with that man?'

Father looked up and at me. 'I now know who that man was. It was Carmichael. He is dead. He died that day.'

Mother, who understood the dead better than Father, went to the front door and turned the open sign to closed. 'Today we clean house, and light incense at the altar. '"

Woolley stood up and went behind the bar. With shaking hands, he began mixing another drink. He was silent; they all were. Daphne looked to him but could say nothing. Clemency went and put her arms around him. "Oh, my love, that was then. War. Nothing made sense. Nothing."

Woolley was visibly shaken, "You can't really just brush it aside, wipe it away like a chalk board. It stays with you, this weight. You have a day when you think, alright, okay, that was a good day. And then it hits. Not a punch, more like your insides liquify and you remember … quite specifically … you killed. Not just soldiers, but mothers and children and animals. For no real reason. You were just told to. And you did."

"Oh, darling." Clemency took Woolley in her arms, her heart bursting. "I think Daphne, we need a rest."

Daphne shook her head. "Yes, I think we all do."

Forgetting dinner, they all went to bed.

Chapter 13

The next morning a letter arrived for them from Mr. Yu. It seems he knew also where they were and sent them a formal invitation to his Great World entertainment palace. As part of the evening, Mr. Yu had arranged a dinner for them and had invited some very special guests. His car would pick them up in the evening around 8 pm.

"What does one wear to such a thing?" Clemency said, looking into the mirror in their room, "This was never mentioned in my Debrett's for Debutantes! There is no section that I can remember about manners for ghostly visitations not to mention visits to sing song palaces and Great World entertainment pavilions, which I am sure is a nice word for a brothel. And no mention whatsoever about how an English rose, such as myself, doesn't swelter in this heat."

Woolley lay on the bed in evening clothes. He felt deflated but game to go on, "Darling, so cynical. We are in Shanghai! Pleasure Palace of the east. Nothing but good clean fun will be had, I am sure of it." He sat up, "Maybe not for the kiddies, but it will be fun. There will be food and drink. There will be places to have our fortunes told.

We can dance. Darling, whatever the bill of fair I will be with you." He got up and crossed the room, placing his hand down Clemency's bare back, "and you are all and the only thing for me."

Clemency smirked.

"Darling," said Woolley, "do I detect a faint frisson of *je ne sais quoi*? Should we not go out on the town tonight?"

"Isn't this town heavily restricted?"

"We will be with the artists, drug takers and criminals, there is no colour bar, no prejudice, just, as I said, good clean fun."

"Hurrah. And what of women. Can I walk freely in this world?"

"Absolutely darling. This is Shanghai, the …!"

"Yes, yes the Paris of the east. Last time I walked in Paris on my own I was catcalled three times and had my bottom pinched."

"I sense our crowd will be on their best behaviour and your bottom will be safe with me," he grinned. "We are in the underworld, the world of misfits. There will be no snobbery tonight." He picked up a warming martini, "To the Empire! May it fade away."

Sensing Woolley was moving into bitterness Clemency stood up and turned. She dropped her dressing gown and naked she said, "Dress me."

Woolley smiled, "With pleasure!"

Chapter 14

Promptly at 8pm a knock came on the shop door. The driver had sent a coolie to tell them that the car was waiting in the street a few blocks away. They were fresh, clean and somewhat rested, and as Daphne was out with friends there was no worry about leaving her alone. Clemency was happy with Woolley's choice – an ivory coloured shift dress with silver embroidery and fringes of glass beads, which shimmered effervescently as she walked. He said she looked like a walking glass of champagne. She laughed but could not help but notice the cloud that hovered over him since Daphne's story. There were so many layers to her complicated fool. How was he able to walk and talk and keep that debonair façade when so haunted? A warm rush came over her, a rush that had been happening more and more frequently. Oh, how in love with him she was. And oh, how she wished she could put him under a glass jar.

They bustled through the early evening crowd behind the man sent to fetch them. "That poor soul," said Clemency. "You can see his whole skeleton. He must be starved."

Woolley had seen thousands like him. There seemed

to be even more now, he thought bitterly, drawn to the city by wars and famine. They came from their farms without an education only to make pittance a day, using half to pay rent on their rickshaw and some place to sleep. What remained was spent on rice in the morning and perhaps now and then a scribe to write home with a little bit of money for the family. Then, eventually, the strain would lead them to the pipe, and the money for rice and sleep and family would all drain away into opium.

Clemency was speaking Cantonese to the man. He responded over his shoulder, pushing the crowd aside as they walked. She turned to Woolley and smiled. "Gui-on is a poetry major at the university."

"What?"

"Yes. He's working the streets to learn about the common man."

Woolley felt somewhat foolish. "So he is not a starving farmer?"

"Quite the opposite."

Gui-on led them to the car. He bowed to Woolley and said something in Cantonese.

He bowed to Clemency and she handed him a rather large tip.

"Care to translate that?"

"He invited us to his next reading; there will be free food and opium."

"Ah, well, I find poetry hard to stomach on a good day but free food…"

"And opium."

"'Till like the trembling golden stalk
Of some long-petalled star, I walk

Through the dark heavens, and the dew
Falls on my eyes and sense thrills through."
"Such a romantic, my Woolley," as she kissed him.

The driver in livery nodded and opened the door of the lovely merlot Daimler Double-Six. Woolley was impressed, as only a few of these limousines had been made, mostly for royalty, and wondered if it was Mr. Yu's quiet way of showing just how wealthy he was. They climbed inside and although still humid, it seemed cool compared to the night outside where the air pressed down like wet sheets. The car's blinds had been pulled down and Woolley sank into the middle of the dark space, his shirt stuck to his back, and sighed.

"We meet again," came a voice from the very back, accented by a cloud of patchouli and stale cigarette smoke. Clemency squealed and jumped. Because the car was equipped with swivel seats, they turned and came face to face with St. Andrew Woodside-Chang.

"Yes, quite!" said Woolley, trying hard not to wince.

"I took the liberty of, how do the Americans say it, catching a lift. Curious phrase," drawled Woodside-Chang, looking quite pleased with himself.

Clemency, trying to ignore Woodside-Chang, lifted the blinds on her window as the elegant ship of a car slipped into a chaotic stream of traffic, both vehicular and human: cars, buses, horses, rickshaws all pullulating with energy, all shouting, jostling and cajoling for their own share of the streets and boulevard. She watched as a Sikh police officer in a red turban stood in the centre of the madness on a raised platform, furiously blowing his whistle while trying to conduct traffic. The city was alive; the shops were busy with customers while people of all ages and races were out on the streets, lit by the glow of neon and the hundreds of red lanterns hung across entire stretches of street.

"And where are you heading?" asked Woolley, dreading the answer.

"Why, to Mr. Yu's dinner of course, although I am most looking forward to what happens after."

Clemency shivered.

Woodside-Change continued, "I have been conversing here with your man Benedict and…"

"What, you here?!" exclaimed Woolley.

They turned to see Benedict facing them from the front seat.

"Oh Benedict, we were wondering where you were," laughed Clemency.

"Actually," said Benedict calmly, "Forgive me for causing any undue stress. I had heard a few – " he paused, "rumours – and wanted to check a few tremors."

Woodside-Chang roared, "Tremors! War, you mean!"

Clemency looked at them, both concerned. "War? With whom?"

"With everyone really, darling," answered Woolley, "but at this moment it is with the Japanese. And drug lords."

"Ha, ha," chortled Woodside-Chang, "It is the drug lords that run this town; my god, they even police it!"

"Anyway sir," said Benedict, "I suggest we wrap up our business here soonish. There are already Japanese ships moored in the harbour."

"Yes," said Woolley, "I noticed that."

It was then both Clemency and Woolley heard a small sigh. They looked back to Woodside-Chang and there beside him in the shadows was a young girl of about 10.

"Ah, yes," he said, "This is my daughter Akimbad," saying Akimbad in an odd theatrical manner. "I named her after the Devil's seventh in command. When she lives up to her name, I call her Bad but mostly we call her Kim."

"Hallo," said Woolley, who was unaccustomed to speaking with children. The colourless girl stared at him expressionlessly.

"Are you having a lovely time?" ventured Clemency, but again there was no response.

Woodside-Chang rumbled, "She's silent most of the time when with new people. She is a holy terror when alone. I'm quite proud of her." He placed a hand on her bare knee and patted her; the girl twitched as if startled.

Woodside-Chang sat back into the darkness of the car with a wheeze. For a brief while there was uncomfortable silence. Woolley so desperately wanted to draw Benedict out, but not in front of their travelling companion, not now.

The passing lights lit the inside of the car, falling on the girl. She did not move. She had no colour, like pale milk. Her hair was light gold, almost white, with a blue silk bow on either side. She stared unsettlingly at Clemency. She was dressed in a white party dress, the style too young for her. She looked nothing of Woodside-Chang. She seemed more like a very evil doll, thought Woolley.

"I know you," the girl said suddenly, sitting forward

and startling all.

"Do you?" asked Clemency, feeling someone should answer.

"Not you, him — Cecil. We were lovers." Woodside-Chang began cackling with laughter.

"Steady on," said Woolley, clearing his throat.

Clemency smiled. "Oh? Was it a tryst or should I be worried?"

"Darling, you know there is only you, my light, my potted palm."

"In a previous life," the girl intoned, "you beat me!" Woodside-Chang was thoroughly amused at just how uncomfortable the girl was making everyone. "I have never forgiven you."

Woolley flushed, "Well, I am sorry. I hope I can make it up to you in this life."

Akimbad sat back in her seat, disappearing again into the shadow cast by her father.

Woolley let out a sigh and said under his breath to Clemency, "'fraid it's going to be that kind of night…"

St. Andrew Woodside-Chang chuckled ominously, then said, "So many Japanese military types out tonight. I shouldn't wonder if we'll face a road block or two."

Not while we are in this car, Woolley thought.

Chapter 15

Woodside-Chang lit one of his offensive smelling cheroots, the sudden flair illuminating his enormous and glistening face. Both Woolley and Benedict rolled down their windows to let in the moist air. The inside atmosphere changed immediately.

The car stopped at an intersection. There was so much neon, the wet and slick black streets were ablaze in colour as were the faces of those inside the car. Voices could be heard shouting in many languages. The food and rancid oil smells that drifted by were both intoxicating and sick-making in equal measures.

Woolley took in his present situation — those about him, these actors in this play. What an interesting and motley crew. Once or twice Woodside-Chang chuckled quietly to himself, while patting his the knee of his daughter, who could be heard mewing faintly as if in song. Woolley stretched his hand and took Clemency's. She clutched back tightly, her hand moist from the heat and, he suspected, the anxiety of being so close to Woodside-Chang. He leaned over and kissed her. "Oxytocin," he whispered.

Woodside-Chang rumbled, "No substitute for opium,

but pleasant when one can get it."

"What does he mean?" asked Clemency.

"Kissing releases oxytocin, a stimulant that gives a sense of well-being. It means we must kiss more often, and more fervently," replied Woolley.

The car was taking them deeper into the older part of the city. Buildings were becoming lower and much closer together, the neon garish and clichéd – floating dragons and Girls! Girls! Girls!

"Could be anywhere really… we would find your mother here for sure," said Woodside-Chang. His daughter giggled in the shadows.

Woolley squeezed Clemency's hand. She squeezed back. Woolley looked at her profile, her gorgeous black hair like raven feathers caught in a breeze.

"Mr. Yu is known for his hospitality," continued Woodside-Chang wetly. "If I am not mistaken, we are being taken to his restaurant in the Hongku district. I am salivating."

"Will we have snake, daddy?" asked Akimbad.

"Daughter, you will have what you like."

"I am pleased," she replied.

"My daughter," he began, "has inherited my love of the exotic. Delicacies are most often wasted on youth, their palate so unrefined, but my daughter was born a connoisseur. Imagine how she lapped up her mother's milk." He patted her again and again she giggled.

Woolley felt a rush of revulsion.

The car slowed to a stop. Without turning around, the driver said, "I can go no further; the restaurant is through this passage on the left."

Not sure how to answer, Woolley said aloud, "Thank you."

"Do not mention it, Mr. Woolley," said the disembodied voice.

Benedict got out and opened the door for Clemency and Woolley.

"Well darling," said Woolley, "shall we portage?"

Benedict cleared his throat, "Perhaps I should go first, sir. This area of town is watched over by the Green Gang."

"Mr. Benedict!" chuffed Woodside-Chang, "This area is the safest part of the city. What manner of man would even think to break the law when the lawless are the rulers? The Green Gang police for the city in exchange for the liberty to run their … businesses … unhindered. Would you want to face the consequences of crossing Big-Eared Du's law enforcement?" He then shifted his bulk and pulled himself out of the car. "Come daughter," he said, extending a huge pink hand into the back.

Despite Woodside-Chang's admonishment, Benedict did not let down his guard. While walking towards the restaurant, Woolley noted that Woodside-Chang was of nodding acquaintance with many of the men and women in the street; those who did not get the nod, shuffled aside or averted their eyes.

The night was still very hot, hotter it seemed than when they set off. Woodside-Chang was sweating profusely, his white linen suit dark with perspiration. He pulled out a large checkered handkerchief and mopped his brow. Benedict remained himself, collected and pale. The temperature seemed to rise even more as they passed through a low archway and entered an odd cul-de-sac. The air was rank with cooking grease and rotting vegetation, but the courtyard was filled with hundreds of red lanterns and even more cages filled with chirping, singing and shouting birds. It was all so overwhelming that Clemency, usually reserved, pulled out her lace hanky and put it over her nose. "Oh darling, Venice."

"Ah, my thoughts wandered there also."

Suddenly a small man began shouting, "Mr. Woolley, Mr. Woolley!" Woolley was startled and walked over to the man, who was dressed in a western suit but wore a bright red fez. He grabbed Woolley by the lapels to pull him close but before Benedict had a chance to react, Woolley pushed the man off. Benedict started to move towards them until Woolley signalled him to stay back.

"You are Cecil Herbert Woolley, yes?" said the little man in an indistinguishable accent.

"I am."

"You are in grave danger, Mr. Woolley. Your friend, Capt. Shaw, has done something terribly wrong."

"As he is dead, I am not sure there is much wrong he could get into now, is there?" drawled Woolley.

"Oohhh, that is where you are wrong, Mr. Woolley!" The man began to giggle uncontrollably. "There is a whole mountain of, how you say, wrong he can get into now."

"See here," Woolley started, eying Benedict to come over and take charge.

"Mr. Woolley, being dead only opens a whole new set of problems. Living is easy while death is, oh, so very complicated," the man giggled again. "Especially to those …" He broke off seeing Benedict walking towards him. "Keep your wits for the days ahead, Mr. Woolley, and protect your goddaughter. And Miss de la Tour. There will be many tribulations in the coming days. I warn you. Tribulations!" He shifted and moved into the crowd, disappearing immediately.

Woolley straightened his jacket.

"Sir?" said Benedict.

"No, no, it's fine, Benedict."

"Did he hurt you?"

"No, no, he was just letting me know that the next few days will be a bit 'bumpy.'"

"Sir, I got the impression he meant more than a 'bit.' Shall I follow him?"

"No, I sense he's served his purpose. I also sense there will be more events like this in the days ahead."

"Darling," said Clemency, coming over to Woolley. "Who was that extraordinary man? He looked like someone straight out of a Berlin café. He might as well have worn a sign around his neck that said 'Shifty.'"

"Ha! Yes, that would suit him well. He had some advice for us."

"Advice?"

"Yes, the general 'keep to the path' type of advice." He paused. "Listen, let's enjoy dinner and see how the evening unfolds."

"Sir," said Benedict, "Mr. St. Andrew Woodside-Chang and his daughter have already gone in. Will you be needing me further tonight?

"No, Benedict, no, although it is always nice to have you around."

"It is my pleasure, always. I would like to wander a little. Ask a few questions."

"Yes. Ask away. Get to know the locals. What makes them tick, or not tick, or even tock."

Benedict nodded, picking up the worried undercurrent in Woolley's voice.

"Darling," Clemency said, taking his arm. "If I weren't so terribly fond of you, I would have you committed."

"No sweeter compliment has ever been paid, thank you my darling."

Benedict wandered off and was swallowed by the throng as he moved back through the archway and out into the night.

"Darling," said Woolley, "shall we put on the nose bag?"

Clemency kissed him gently and they crossed the crowded square.

The restaurant was in an old house that would have been perfectly at home in the French Concession. A mix of colonial and local architecture, it was 3 storeys high with a pagoda slant to its roof and French doors leading out onto a second-floor balcony with railings reminiscent of a Chinese screen. The red light of the lanterns highlighted the peeling paint on the pillars that surrounded the porch, and a new menu had been plastered over an old one that sat by the stairs that led up to the front door. The door itself was made of steel, better suited for a bank vault than a home. It was covered with rivets and bolts and festooned with ornamental bric-a-brac and filigree, dragons and mountains, rivers and Taoists. Woolley reached out but before he could touch it, unseen hands from within swung it open. They were immediately hit by an ungodly blast of crowd chatter, jazz, delicious smells and an inferno of heat.

"Goodness!" Clemency exclaimed. "Makes outside seem like Switzerland."

Woolley smiled faintly, "No place like home," and gestured Clemency in, the doors closing noiselessly behind them.

The entrance still felt like it belonged to a house, with a large ornate stairwell on the left rising to the second floor, but everything else homey was removed and made useful as a serving establishment. The original would have been of Western design but was now filtered through Shanghai tastes. The wood was an elegant and gleaming black, the wallpaper a flocked red and gold dragon design. The rooms were divided by screens with the same design as the balcony railings, and incense burned below an altar that contained a painting of the Buddha, a photo of an elderly matriarch, and a china sculpture of a dog cocking its leg as if about to pee. There was a small porcelain bowl filled with nuts and a sad mandarin orange. A uniformed man with shining black hair plastered back with pomade stood behind a tall stand, a reservation book open, a brush in his hand. He sized up Woolley and Clemency, then spoke in English without a hint of accent, "Are you expected?"

"Yes, it seems we are. At least, I hope we are," said Woolley. "The name is Woolley; we are guests of Mr. Yu."

The mention of Mr. Yu caused the man to stiffen as if run through with a small electrical charge. "Indeed, Mr. Woolley and Miss de la Tour, you are expected. The other members of your party have already been seated," He rang a small bell so suddenly and violently that Clemency jumped. A small man appeared. In Mandarin he told the man, "Mr. Yu's party, please seat them well and do not wait for a tip." He then turned to Woolley and with a smile said, "Fang Yi will take you to dinner. Your party is in a private room. The chef has been all day preparing for this auspicious event." He then bowed. "An honour Mr. Woolley, Miss de la Tour."

"Honour's ours," said Woolley, somewhat over-whelmed and ever so slightly worried.

In a very thick accent Fang Yi said, "Follow please."

He pulled back a red velvet curtain fringed in gold that was covering a small doorway. This must have been a servant's passage, thought Woolley, as they walked down a narrow hall decidedly different from the en-trance, this much more European. Perhaps it remained Western as a bit of exotica. A painting of Queen Victoria caught Woolley's eye. "Ma'am," he said, clicking his heels. Clemency frowned.

There was a cacophony of sound coming from the door at the end of the hall, mixed with a heavenly smell of incense and spices. It was also hellishly hot with no mov-ing air. Woolley could feel a stream of perspiration run down the middle of his back. The man in front opened the door then turned and bowed, "Here, please."

There was a narrow half flight of stairs, poorly lit by small sconces. The air was foggy with atmosphere. Woolley went first, then reached back and stroked Clemency's arm to ground him. She took his hand and kissed it. Reaching the top of the stairs, they were both surprised to see it was a grand library. It was octagonal in shape, with ornate glassed-in shelves around six of the eight walls holding what looked like hundreds, if not thousands, of books. In the centre, awash in fiscus and statuary, was an enormous table. Around that table sat an assortment of Chinese businessmen, diplomats, persons of note and St. Andrew Woodside-Chang. Woodside-Chang glowed in a food- induced sheen while his daughter ran about the room making a jabbering yipping sound, much to the shock and consternation of the gathered crowd.

"Mr. Woolley!" shouted Mr. Yu, and stood up wiping his hands on a napkin. "You are here, and the lovely Miss de la Tour, here also! You madam, if you will accept the opinion of someone so worthless as me, have grown more radiant since last we met! More radiant!"

"Good lighting and a night's sleep," smiled Clemency, somewhat flustered.

"Yes, well," said Woolley. "Here we are!"

"Yes, here you are, Mr. Woolley," croaked Woodside-Chang like a toad, his mouth full of food. "Come sit, eat. Excellent, excellent."

"Mr. Woolley, Miss de la Tour," Mr. Yu continued, "I have seated you beside Madame Yi, who m of course you know."

"Goodness!" said Woolley, "I know you only through reputation and your films of course." An intensely elegant, pale woman turned to them both. She was wearing a tightly-fitted red cheongsam richly embroidered in gold bats and coins. She closed her eyes slowly, then opened them. She nodded curtly to Woolley, then with eyes smouldering, took Clemency's hand and kissed it.

"And Mr. Woolley and Miss de la Tour," Mr. Yu interrupted enthusiastically, "please be introduced to my other honoured guests. May I introduce –

Foreign Minister Zhang." A nod.

"Celebrated poet Zu Xi Peng."

"Charmed," he replied.

"Ambassador Leung," who belched quite loudly.

"Esteemed local businessman Hu Shi." Bowing, he replied, "An honour."

This continued another seven times until he had introduced most of the people around the table. Both Clemency and Woolley were so overwhelmed by the quantity of people, not to mention the heat, they remembered none of the names or occupations. They knew it wouldn't matter.

"And, of course your, and my, esteemed friend Moffat St. Andrew Woodside-Chang and his lovely daughter." A loud rrrrrrrr then came from under Madam Li's chair. She yelped and stood up. It was Akimbad brandishing a lobster. Mr. Yu smiled with self-satisfaction, as if he'd pulled off the society coup of the season and managed to get a Tatler photographer to capture it all.

"Yes," said Woolley, "It is an honour and a pleasure to be here and to dine with what certainly must be the glowing lights of Shanghai society." He felt faint. Clemency pinched him on the bottom. The guests looked on, confused at the behaviour of these Western barbarians.

Benedict, conspicuously inconspicuous, made his way through the crowd, following the strange man who had warned Woolley. His furtiveness reminded Benedict of a rat as he skittered ahead, darting into doorways, glancing every which way then moving quickly on, giving the sense he was searching out a rat hole, a safe place to hide. He kept looking over his shoulder to the right, expecting someone, his odd and frightened face slick with perspiration under the glow of the neon lights. Surely he saw Benedict, or did he? Benedict assumed they were mutually aware of each other and were playing a game of cat and mouse, or in this case, cat and rat. The man paused as he came upon a darkened alley fronted by a half-heartedly built wooden fence and gate, plastered with revolutionary tracts and posters. He looked across the street, confirming the game by making direct eye contact with Benedict, then opened the gate and scurried down the passage.

Benedict thought two things: "He's leading me into a trap," and "do I follow him, aware of that?"

He followed.

He crossed the sea of people to the other side of the street and pushed open the gate. The alley was dark, the tall clay brick walls of the buildings blocking any light that wanted to get in. The air was close and motionless and stank of garbage and urine. Benedict adjusted his senses. He always had excellent night vision but in this odd atmospheric swamp he could not focus; he felt like he was swimming in black ink. He moved forward, barking his shin against something, then kicking something else, something soft and rotten. In front there was only blackness, behind him also. He was unsettled. Suddenly there was a click and about 10 meters ahead a blast of yellow light shot out into the alley from an opened door. A shape moved in front of the door then darkness again as the door closed. Benedict ran in the direction of the light. He heard a flurry of wings, felt the swish of air on his face but saw nothing. Then, mid-step, he was seized by what felt like arms encircling him and could move no more.

Woodside-Chang made a gnawing sound. "This is snake! Think of it Mr. Woolley, only minutes ago this creature was slithering, full of life, in a dark box surrounded by other snakes, also slithering and full of life. Now he is in pieces before me. Excellent, excellent."

Clemency felt ill. Woolley winced, smiled and said, "Vegetarianism is becoming more and more appealing."

"Come, come Mr. Woolley," continued Woodside-Chang. "The Chinese believe, as many superior cultures do, that a life consumed is a life not wasted. And are we not, as I am sure you would have to agree, Miss de la Tour, certainly the most superior of species?" He was extremely pleased with himself and raised a glass to those present.

Clemency sipped her tea.

"I'm afraid I have to disagree," she said. "Here we are around the table, all talented, educated, elegantly-dressed, shall I say worldly people, but I count five types of rare animal on this table; beautiful animals now dead. And yet we have no compassion for them save how they taste, perhaps the rarity of them, caring about what we own, what we have conquered. There is rumour that there will be another war. I see some of the gentlemen here are already in uniform." Woolley put his hand on Clemency's lap. "Did we not learn anything from the war that just passed? We so respect the soldier, the general, the warrior but what was everyone fighting for? It was greed and ego and profit. Mostly profit. Just to have more. More than what we need. More empty rooms. It's all a game with made-up rules. Men playing like children, dressing up. It's all lunacy. Superior species? No! This species, our species, our civilization is the most uncivilized…"

A young man in uniform cleared his throat. "Humble respect. Wouldn't you say we should stand by our motherland? Shouldn't we defend our beliefs, our custom, our way of life?"

Clemency, flushing red and glistening from the heat, began, "All of that is made up. It's not real."

"What then," the young man asked earnestly, "do you believe in?" The men at the table began to chortle. Clemency was suddenly very tired.

"I believe in beauty," she said quietly, "and Cecil."

Zu Xi Peng leaned over to Woolley and whispered, "I hope your mistress is much more silent and much less opinionated."

Chapter 16

Benedict knew struggling was out of the question, the grip was too strong and not quite human. He soon became aware of another presence in the darkness, and then a voice, "Kindly remain silent, Mr. Woolley." His captor reeked of damp mold, like a root cellar or … a crypt.

Benedict stiffened, "I am not Woolley."

"Ah, then you must be Mr. Benedict. No matter, it is neither of you we are interested in per se." Benedict could not place the accent. Hong Kong, or perhaps England. "We would like you to inform the girl, the daughter of Captain Shaw, that we have … shall we say … a proposition for her."

"A proposition? I do not understand."

"Sir, come, come, you have been around long enough, you have been through wars, you know just how low one can go to get what one needs. Captain's Shaw's daughter has something we need. She must give it to us. It is as simple as that, or there will be consequences."

Benedict felt sickened, "And what is the proposition?"

"That is the proposition, although you could call it a little one-sided."

"Why should she comply? Is this a threat?"

"Threat? Oh Mr. Benedict. The word 'threat' seems so mild. Perhaps we should show you, put an image into your head of what will happen if she does not comply."

There was another voice now. "It is forbidden … he will gain knowledge he should not have."

"Precisely, precisely. We want him to understand the seriousness of her not complying. The exquisite, horrific fate that is in store for her."

Benedict's mind started racing, "How dare you threaten … "

"As I said before, I am not 'threatening.' The door."

Benedict's insides became liquid. In the darkness there was a knock, a strange rapping upon the door. Seconds later a metal latch could be heard turning and the door in front of him began to open.

A blast of molten hot air hit him. Light slashed out, so bright and unexpected. His eyes slowly adjusted. What was before him was so horrific in its enormity, so horrible that he could not quite comprehend it. Then, as if someone had switched on the wireless and played it at full volume, came the roar of fire and the screams of thousands.

"Look, Mr. Benedict. See what your Miss Shaw has brought upon her ancestors? Shaming her family. Look, Mr. Benedict."

Benedict tried to look away but couldn't. There, in this hellish infinite space, were thousands upon thousands of skeletal people, all holding begging bowls, all moaning, screaming for food. Shuffling slowly in groups, in rows, in lines, flesh hanging off their bone arms. They were being followed by huge bloated creatures dressed in fancy court costumes, their faces melting with the rippling of the heat, their huge maws drooling. Methodically they were peeling the skin off the beggars and eating the flesh. The skin would come off in wet dripping strips and the creatures would raise the strips to their lips and slurp them in like noodles. Laughing to themselves or each other. Pointing out the fleshier ones, chasing after them, peeling off skin.

"Why are you showing me this?!" gasped Benedict.

"Why?" The voice mocked, "For you to remember, Mr. Benedict. For you to take back with you and pass along to young Miss Shaw. She must comply or this is her fate. Her parents are already in there, somewhere, and if she does not relent, she will be also." The voice started laughing, loud and manically, then the door slammed shut and the heat and the screaming and the blinding light were gone. There was silence, almost worse, then the grip faded, and he stumbled and fell into the blackness.

Chapter 17

Benedict felt a hand on his shoulder. He opened his eyes to find Woolley standing over him, looking concerned.

"Benedict," said Woolley. "Why are you lying here? Are you ill? Good god, you are shaking."

He was back at the restaurant.

"Clemency," continued Wooley, "hail a conveyance, we must get Benedict home."

"Seems more drunk than anything," grumbled Woodside-Chang.

"Or opium!" piped up Akimbad.

Woodside-Chang chortled, "Naughty girl."

After much discussion and disagreement, Benedict convinced Woolley and Clemency to continue with their night. He would say nothing to them of his evening until they were alone. There was a reason they were invited to Mr. Yu's establishment and Benedict felt it was important that they find out why. He also needed to go find Daphne.

As the rickshaw drove off, Benedict pale and ill inside it, Woolley sighed. "I fear this evening has only just begun."

"Yes, I too fear it," agreed Clemency.

Woolley lit two cigarettes and gave one to her. "Did

you see Benedict's face? He's had a shock. I have never seen him so pale, and he is positively Norwegian in hue at his flushest."

Mr. Yu had two rikshaws waiting. Woolley and Clemency climbed into one while Woodside-Chang and his daughter squeezed into the other. Mr. Yu had come out of the restaurant to give directions to the drivers. He turned and smiled at Woolley. In the garish neon of the street his face took on a sinister look. Woolley hoped it was merely an unfortunate trick of the light. "Do not pay these devils, they are under my employment for the night," instructed Mr. Yu. "An exciting night ahead, Mr. Woolley. I can guarantee many pleasures for you and Miss de la Tour. I must tend to my other dinner guests. I shall take my car and meet you there." He bowed and then encouraged the rickshaw drivers to make haste. Clemency wrapped her arm around Woolley for comfort.

"Damn it all," mumbled Woolley when he knew they were far enough away from Mr. Yu.

Clemency smiled wanly. "I can't help thinking this night is cursed, that we are being used for something. Honestly Cecil, we should just gather up Daphne and leave this place."

The rickshaw jostled to avoid a speeding car flying the flags of some Japanese dignitary. "Damn fool!" shouted Woolley. He sat back and said darkly, "There is certainly much tension in the air tonight." Clemency continued to hold him, despite the horrific humidity, and in silence they watched humanity rush by.

It felt late though in reality it wasn't yet midnight. The city had shifted its excitements for the night and sensing that, Woolley became weary. The train ride, the confusion, the noise, the ghosts, the unsettled sleep, all sat upon him like some tremendous weight. He felt all in; he was tired of waking up each day, of pushing forward. He was weary of the pushing. The convincing. He didn't like what he saw in the mirror. He didn't like what he read in the news. How in this modern age, after such a huge and bloody travesty, nothing was learned? People were money mad. Power mad. All his friends were dead and here he was, still going on.

He remembered the Armistice. November 11, 1918. Walking to a dinner that had been arranged weeks earlier. Who knew the date would be so auspicious? At the time it was the only night everyone had been available and in town, on leave, on furlough. Alexander, who was hosting the dinner, had been discharged and was recovering from wounds sustained in France. Woolley had been demobbed the week before and was still in his uniform as he had no other clothes to wear; his flat had been bombed and burned. Now bells were ringing, people were in the streets, British people, dancing with a bittersweet joy. Who wins in a war, really? The only joy was that it had stopped. When the bells began to ring that morning, carrying the news of peace from parish to parish, city to city, everyone cheered – but Woolley only felt a deflating sense of relief. Suddenly a woman rushed up to him, giving him a hug, her eyes laughing. He smiled back but inside he felt nothing but bitterness. His was a generation that had had their youth stolen, their dreams dashed, their innocence taken. No more could he innocently kiss a girl in a library, listen to opera, or hold his breath at the beauty of nature or human inventiveness. It was now all tarnished, flaked with corrosion. But for a few, all the friends he had started school with were now ghosts, reaching out, open-eyed, wanting to be trivial one more time.

He pushed on, caught in the crowd, its intensity swelling. Someone drunkenly tried to set the base of Nelson's column on fire. The air was cool and misted with fog, cigarettes, alcohol, sweat.

Upon arrival at Alexander's flat, he rang the bell. "Hallo!" a voice shouted above the noise of the crowd. He looked up to see Harry Fine and Alexander Button-Smith in civilian clothes, not their own, smoking cigarettes on the balcony while watching the madness. "Come up! The lock stopped working ages ago." The door opened with some difficulty as it had been hastily repaired, though it was still splintered and scorched in places. Rubble lay in the stairwell, lit by every light in the building. All the doors of all the flats were open and the occupants were going from room to room holding tea cups and tumblers of what looked like gin. Harry stuck his head out of the door to Alex's flat. "Hallo, old bean!" He reached out and hugged Woolley, holding him longer than gentlemanly, both just enjoying the fact they could. "No use to anyone at all right now, I'm afraid," said Harry quietly, and stood back. Woolley realized the hug was a way to avoid the shaking of hands, for Harry had only one. "Will get a bally metal claw or something. Looking forward to that," Harry said, seeing Woolley registering the missing hand. "Might take a while, not a priority. 'Funny thing' … here, come in, let me take your coat … 'Funny thing', I said to the doctor chap – kindest man I'd ever met. I said, jokingly, 'I say, doc, will I ever play the piano again? Gave me such joy and all.'"

"Why Harry, you could barely tie your shoes, let alone play a piano," laughed Woolley.

"I know! All thumbs. Ha, well, thumb now. Nothing of that musical sort. Said it to lighten the mood as the doctor looked so sad. Well damned if you know it, the next day the fellow comes in beaming, a package all tied up in string in his arms. 'Piano-for-the-left-hand sheet music!' he tells me. He was so proud of himself. I nearly died there and then." He sipped his gin, "There are still good people, Cecil." He drifted. "Anyway! Now I have all the sheet music for the left hand one could want."

Woolley beamed at Harry and hugged him again. "Harry," he said, as they walked into the front sitting room, "it was a dark day when His Majesty's government gave you a gun. What were they thinking?!"

"Ah, you forget, Woolley old bean, I'm a crack shot, one thing I can do. Shoot grouse. It's in the blood."

"Woolley!" Shouted Alex Button-Smith as he climbed through the balcony window. As he turned, Woolley saw that he had a large scar across one side of his face and a black eye patch. "Quite the racket, eh? You'd think the war had ended or something!" He said this in his usual dry sardonic way and shook Woolley's hand aggressively with much back-slapping. "Look at all the punters out there dancing. Can't begrudge them, but nothing is solved; only thing we learned was how to mow down chaps more efficiently. Quite a party, though." He took Woolley's hand again, "How are you, chum? What will you do now in civvy street?" Button-Smith was a teacher at a boy's prep. He continued, "Wonder if there will be anyone left to teach? And how can I wade through the old algebra after what we've seen? What we've been through? I know these are early days. Time heals and all that. But the bitterness in me is palpable, like muck in my mouth. You were in the air, weren't you? I was in the trenches with old Harry here. Mostly mud and horses screaming … "

Chapter 18

"Woolley!" Clemency shook him, "Where were you just now?"

Startled, Woolley took in a deep humid breath and exhaled, "I was in Alexander Button-Smith's apartment, Armistice day. A dinner party far away from here."

"Sounds lovely," Clemency sat back. "I was at a weekend shooting party at Castle Howard, of all places. I hid in the orangery, as I have not ever seen the 'sport' in blood sports or the joy, really, in any sport. Which is why I love you, dear Woolley."

"Ha! Yes! I have no desire to put my ball in anyone else's net, except yours of course." Woolley kissed Clemency's hand as the rickshaw pulled up in front of a monstrous building with pillars topped by roaring stone dragons, each holding a red lantern.

"We have arrived, Mr. Woolley, Miss de la Tour," said the driver, surprising them both with his English. "Forgive me, please, my humble and ignorant opinion, I am just a rickshaw driver, but this is not a place for foreigners. Here you are 'fan kuei'. You will come away with pockets full of stones where you once had gold."

Woolley smiled, taking the driver's advice seriously.

He slipped him some money, which the man gratefully accepted.

"Oh Cecil … !" cried Clemency. He turned to see a crowd of eyeless beggars moving en masse towards them, alms bowls in hands.

Woolley quickly took Clemency's arm. "Shall we?"

"We haven't a choice, it seems," she replied. "Oh darling, the places we go."

As they began to walk towards the stairs of The Grand World, Woolley stopped Clemency to kiss her. "We are all in the gutter, darling …" he began, "Oh, how I love you. I cannot imagine being able to function without you. darling?"

"Yes, Cecil?"

"You've made me respectable."

"Not that, Woolley!" she laughed.

"Yes, I'm afraid so. Do you still find me fascinating when I've become so …" he searched, "the peg? Darling… would you ever consider … ?"

"Ah, young love!" drawled Woodside-Chang, stepping out of the shadows. "I had come out for what passes as fresh air in this city. There is certainly none in there. It's also hotter out here, I fear." He lit one of his cheroots and blew acrid smoke over their heads. "Your rickshaw took much longer to get here than mine. Were you waylaid?" Woolley stiffened, his dislike for the man growing with each encounter.

Clemency gripped Woolley's arm tightly, then let go to open her bag and bring out two cigarettes, which Woolley lit. "Where is your lovely daughter?" she asked.

"Sent her home. She was liable to be sold to the highest bidder in this place," Woodside-Chang chortled.

"Sent her home alone?" asked Clemency, worriedly.

He smiled. "How charming your concern. However, my daughter is perfectly capable of taking care of herself."

"She is only a child and this city …" countered Clemency.

"Child, yes, but honestly around that child we should worry about our own safety," said Woolley quietly under his breath.

Woolley stubbed out his cigarette and looked up. "Seems quite a hopping spot."

"An understatement, Mr. Woolley. This is the Grand World. On the first floor are gaming tables, singsong girls, magicians, pick-pockets, slot machines, fireworks, birdcages, fans, stick incense, acrobats, and ginger. The next floor seethes with actors, crickets and cages, pimps, midwives, barbers, and earwax extractors. The third has jugglers, herb medicines, ice cream parlours, and very young girls in gowns slit to reveal their lack of hips. The fourth floor has shooting galleries, fan-tan tables, massage benches, dried fish and intestines, and dance platforms. The fifth features girls with dresses slit to the armpits, a stuffed whale, storytellers, balloons, peep shows, masks, a mirror maze, scribes, rubber goods, and a temple. On the top floor and roof are tightrope walkers, Chinese checkers, mah-jongg, firecrackers, lottery tickets, marriage brokers and sin, sin and more sin. Sin, Miss de la Tour."

Clemency stepped back. "I am familiar with the term."

"Ah!" roared Woodside-Chang. "Here, behind these walls, sin is raised to an art form."

"My honoured guests!" shouted Mr. Yu, running down the front steps, his hands clapping with delight. "Welcome to my humble place of business! Please come inside, come inside!" A girl who could be no more than ten came forward from nowhere, holding a basket of flowers. She pinned one on Woolley and Clemency, Woodside-Chang already having one. "These flowers will mark you as my guest," Mr. Yu said. "You will be treated with the upmost care." He bowed.

"Ah," said Woolley, wondering how non-flower-wearing people were treated. He and Clemency followed Mr. Yu. "Darling," whispered Woolley into Clemency's ear, "where to begin? I confess I would prefer just to skip right to the end when we are in a car and travelling homeward. No, better still, home."

Woodside-Chang came up to them. "Come lovebirds, Mr. Yu has given us a table and some privacy. We can enjoy the show and be served free drinks, although I suspect with less alcohol than those of the paying guests."

"Show?" asked Clemency.

"Lily-footed sing-song girls of the Foochow Road, I am sure. But what better floor show than the humanity that throngs the loins of this palace of iniquity?"

"You seem to have quite the contempt for human-kind, Mr. St. Andrew Woodside-Chang," said Clemency.

"Miss de la Tour, we are old friends now. Isn't it about time you started calling me Moffatt ?"

"I can't believe the world is all bad," she said, reaching for Woolley's hand.

Woodside-Chang glanced at her with a look that said,

'wait and see for yourself.' Clemency held on to Woolley's hand as they made their way forward. "I have such a bad feeling about this," she whispered.

"As do I, as do I."

Chapter 19

Mr. Yu came over to their table and sat down, giving them an indulgent smile. "Miss de la Tour, we should put you under glass, how delicate you are."

"I am not a flower, Mr. Yu," Clemency said, with a touch of indignance.

"Far from it!" said Mr. Yu, fearing he had insulted his guest. "You have English brine and bony structures!"

Woolley smiled. Clemency frowned.

Oh!" cried Mr. Yu, quickly changing the subject. "It is Madame Yi! Madame Yi! Yoohoo! Madame Yi! Whatever could she be doing here? You must excuse me. I must welcome her to my unworthy establishment."

"She is alone," said Clemency.

"A cold fish," said Woolley. "Alluring though rather bony."

Clemency laughed, "Bony ? Honestly darling, you are a …"

Woolley waved his hand, "Don't say it, I know, a wonder. I am a wonder. The doctor said so and now it's gone to my head."

Woodside-Chang scraped his chair and got up. "I must find the facilities. If they have them."

A waiter brought iced drinks in tumblers. Woolley placed his hands around his, while Clemency sipped hers.

"Oh, darling, try this, it is delicious."

"Looks fruity," said Woolley in mock horror. Clemency laughed.

Looking at her, he asked, "Do you wonder why all this attention is being lavished on us? We are nobodies in this world. Woodside-Chang and Mr. Yu are being so attentive. Certainly, there are other westerners they can wine and dine."

"Perhaps this has something to do with Daphne and the strange parade of characters that have been showing up at her shop," mused Clemency.

"Well yes, agreed, but what is it about that shop that would be so? Quaint as it is, I cannot imagine people rushing to get into the tea room racket."

"What if it isn't the shop, but the location?"

"The cramped alley?"

"Yes, what if there is something there that they want? It is an odd location. Have you noticed all the symbols carved about? And in the cobblestones. Have you noticed how the main of the house is slightly askew to its outer self?"

"Darling, you noticed all of this in the past 48 hours since we've gotten here?" asked an impressed Woolley.

"I am the brains in this outfit, darling, but in all honesty Daphne told me most of it. Her father apparently went on about it once. Kept the altar going. Fresh persimmons on it every day. Joss sticks."

"I see," said Woolley as he intertwined his fingers with hers on the table.

A jazz band started up and the crowd cheered, rushing to the dance floor. Mr. Yu returned with Madam Yi in tow. He was beaming with pride. "You remember Madame Yi from the dinner, Miss de la Tour, Mr. Woolley."

Woolley stood. "How could I forget, charmed once again."

Madame Yi ignored him and turned to Clemency, taking her hand but this time not kissing it. Clemency was struck at how cool to the touch her hand was, like she had been holding an iced drink. "One could never forget Miss de la Tour," Madame Yi said in a very quiet and strangely childish voice. "Oh, how too extraordinary to meet again. When you left I was instantly saddened. My unworthy heart beat harder." She then, rather over-dramatically Woolley thought, put her hand on her heart. Clemency noticed just how low cut her dress was, her nipples erect under the slight fabric, and felt very uncomfortable.

Mr. Yu, sensing an awkward silence, cleared his throat. "Perhaps you could sit at our humble table for a moment and share a cocktail with us?"

Madame Yi put her hand to her forehead and sat down in Mr. Yu's seat. He cleared his throat and snapped his fingers for someone to bring him another chair. Madame Yi took Clemency's hand from across the table. "I know we are going to be such grand friends."

Mr. Yu arranged his chair and sat down. "Now," he said to Woolley, "may I order us some drinks, more drinks? Then I must show you my unworthy establishment, however unremarkable it is."

"Come, come Mr. Yu," said Woolley, taking in the crush of dancers, the band, the floor- to-ceiling madness.

"I'm not an expert in all things night-club, but it seems to me you have quite the place here."

Mr. Yu smiled toothfully. "It pays the bills, serves the needs. But I long for a place of more refined culture. Someplace where Europeans – and please, I mean no offense, but – someplace where Europeans … ah … would not come."

Woolley sipped his drink and frowned. "Well yes, my people can be a tad tiresome. But why not … ?"

"For everyone?"

"Quite."

"Perhaps. I am in a forgiving mood tonight. Such lovely people. Such illustrious people."

The band slipped into a new song.

"Oh Woolley," sighed Clemency, "The foxtrot."

"Shall we?" He put out his arm. "If you will excuse us." Woolley said to the company. Woodside-Chang was just returning and waved his hand in approval.

Woolley and Clemency began to dance. Woolley was, as always, forever struck by the firmness of Clemency. The realness of her presence. Her muscles so taught, her skin, her makeup, her sinew, her lovely skin. He ran his hand down her spine to the small of her back and contemplated eternity.

"Oh, darling," Clemency chuckled. Woolley followed her gaze. It was Woodside-Chang watching them with satisfaction, while two young girls sat on either side.

"Darling, are they … ?"

"Yes, I believe they are cleaning his ears. They are ear wax girls."

Clemency closed her eyes for a moment. "No," she

grinned, "I will never be able to ever clear that image from my memory."

"Welcome to Shanghai, darling," he laughed. "Ah! Another foxtrot." Woolley took charge and slowly danced Clemency off the dance floor and over to what appeared to be a brass bird cage but was in fact a very ornate and exquisite elevator. He pulled her close and whispered, "Sugar," then kissed her passionately. She tasted of salt. Somewhere a bell rang. "Ah!" he exclaimed, "True love!" The door of the elevator began to open. They stepped back out of the way only to be ushered from behind by Mr. Yu into the sumptuous box. "May I show you the more, shall we say, exclusive parts of my establishment?"

"How could we say no?" asked Woolley, and took Clemency's hand. "Darling?"

Mr. Yu, puffed with pride, began to close the outer door when someone shouted, "Wait, do wait!" It was Madame Yi.

"Why, Madame Yi!" cooed Mr. Yu. "We are honoured to share a car with you! You find us about to embark on a little private tour; would it be presumptuous of me to ask if you'd like to join us?" Madame Yi entered the elevator box and lightly brushed against Clemency. "I would be delighted."

Mr. Yu leaned forward and brought the outer door to a close. Gears whirred and chains clattered. "This is absolutely the most modern in all of Shanghai, all safety and elegance. Everything shipshape, as you English like to say."

Woolley stiffened. He thought it a bad sign to be told something is safe. Was it not safe before? He stood slightly a moment and then said, "The tide."

"What, darling?" asked Clemency.

"Shipshape and Bristol fshion. Bristol has quite a bustling port, many goods in and out. The tide was strong and emptied the port and with each low tide the ships moored there were stranded, causing tremendous stress on the ships' hulls. As the port was such an important one, shipbuilders began to fashion boards that sat more upright out of water at low tide. So, if the cargo was not stored safely, in Bristol fashion, with the low tide and the harbour rats, … well!"

"Thank you for that history lesson, Woolley," said Clemency, patting him as they ascended to the top floor.

Chapter 20

The night continued to be hot, the air wet, like standing next to steam. Daphne unhitched her bicycle and pushed it a while along the walk. Streetlights were not lit, and the path between the houses that she used to get to the main street was eerily quiet and still. No sounds at all, not even insects, just the sound of her feet upon the gravel and the rolling of her tires. The walls backing onto the path were aged and stained, and covered with patches of night-blooming stock that had escaped from the gardens behind. The scent was intoxicating, and she paused to breath it in: nicotiana, jasmine, lily, the sweetest of night scents. A cluster of bats skittered above her. A slight breeze came up, rustling her skirt.

Daphne was thinking of the evening that had just past. She was the kind of person who replayed everything, looking for errors and missteps, always judging herself harshly – and tonight was no exception. She was happy with the set of friends she had found quite by chance, of how they accepted her when her mixed race was a problem to so many in the city. But still, all these new friends were from other places, the sons and daughters of diplomats and foreign business people who didn't give a fig about race, or not as much as they did elsewhere. Like Chester, who was Ceylonese and Irish. It was just so nice to be able to focus on things other than who your parents were and what they did and their place in society.

Willow branches hung low here and brushed the top of her head. A rat scurried in front of her. She was passing now through the labyrinthine market streets which led out of the concession, usually bustling at this time of night with travellers and lovers but now strangely empty. The sky was indigo, the stars pressing down, unlike in the centre of the city where the only light at night was manmade. She walked onto a main road. The dry dirt of the ground dusted up in tiny clouds around her feet. She crossed the road and entered a small ornamental park with a gurgling fountain. Soon she would be passing through a gate, literally the wall that divided the International from the French concession. It was custom to linger here and gossip but tonight the park was quiet.

She stopped. Faintly in the distance, a bell was ringing. At first, she thought it must be a wind chime but no, it was too rhythmic. She started forward but stopped after a few paces. It was getting closer and with it came a new sound, a thud as if someone was stamping a pole onto the ground. Perhaps a beggar ringing a bell or tapping a cane. She continued walking through the park towards a copse of trees that were now just a dark huddle of shapes in the night, her head still full of the evening's events. On the other side was the gate to the street that lead to her neighbourhood. There though, in the darkness, she saw movement, something white. She hesitated. Should she worry? Was she in danger? Should she hide? She struggled to make out what was there; what was moving and so rhythmically?

The moon appeared and cast sickly half-shadows across the grass in front of her. Walking towards her was a Taoist priest in ceremonial robes holding a staff with a bell on it, striking the earth as he walked. She sighed. Just a priest. But then she noticed movement behind him: shadows – five shadows that jumped each time the priest struck his cane on the ground. She looked on and as the shadows became clearer, she realized with sudden horror what was ahead of her. A corpse walker, a corpse walker returning the dead. The five corpses stood in a straight line, arms at their sides, and then jumped forward with each thump of the cane. Upon their foreheads was a yellow paper, a spell to reanimate and pacify them. It was horrifying to see, the putrefying dead – jumping, following the priest. The line was heading in her direction, but she was too terrified to move. As they came closer, she saw that two of the corpses were headless: a man and a woman, each holding the other's head in their hands. With a shock so intense she cried out — the headless corpses were her parents!

The priest, hearing her, held up his arm and the procession stopped. He eyed her in the darkness. Daphne could smell the rot, see that the priest too was a corpse, green in pallor and made of mostly bone, his vestments hanging and full of holes. He pointed a finger at her. "You," he said and stamped his pole, ringing the bell. All the corpses jerked slightly, and with the movement the yellow slips of paper fell from their foreheads. Gradually the figures started to awake, blink, become aware, and with that awareness they all began to scream as the absolute horror of their situation set in. Daphne put her hands to her ears; it was a heartbreaking sound, the screaming so loud that she couldn't shut it out. Her dead parents, there in front of her, wailing and gnashing from severed heads. Her mother, her head in her father's arms, began crying, "Daphne, Daphne, what is happening?"

"Oh mummy, mummy," she cried, tears streaming down her face.

"Those men! Those men are doing this, Daphne!"

"Men? What men? Oh mummy!"

"Listen to them! They have your Father and me ; we cannot move on. Daphne, why? We have no place to live. You didn't give us a house to live in !"

"But mummy you didn't want a traditional funeral!"

"We have no food! We are starving! Give the men what they want. The men!"

"What men?" Daphne was beside herself now, screaming, "Mummy!" and holding her hands over her ears, crying and shaking. Then suddenly there was silence and Daphne collapsed onto the grass. In the distance, crickets began to sing.

Chapter 21

The elevator shuddered to a halt about six inches above the floor. Mr Yu blushed, "Still learning." He cranked the elevator handle back and the lift chunked down so that it was level with the floor. "Humble apology," said Mr. Yu quietly as he slid back the filigree brass work door and motioned for everyone to step out. They entered a wide balcony with numerous doors on the inside wall and a vast opening on the other, a magnificent "O" which gave a 180-degree view of the entire establishment below. The clamour was incredible; smoke funneled up in front of them like a twister. Woolley and Clemency walked to the ornate banister and peered down. What a marvel, Woolley thought, as he touched Clemency gently. The crowd below glistened in the artificial light; dancers, drinkers, diners, acrobats and gamblers. Music swelled and billowed, the sound of traditional Chinese and jazz. There was movement on every level. So much colour, so much wealth. But to Clemency and Woolley there was also something else that could be felt rising in that twirling cloud of blue smoke. Something low and evil and rotten.

"Oh, darling," Clemency said faintly, grabbing tightly onto Woolley.

"Yes, me too," answered Woolley, reading her

thoughts.

"Mr. Woolley, Miss de la Tour," shouted Mr. Yu. "Come let me show you my aquarium!"

Madame Yi floated over and took Clemency's arm. "Yes, let us all go see Mr. Yu's aquarium!"

Mr. Yu led them the short distance down the balcony to one of many similar unmarked doors. He slid a panel to reveal an enormous room, nearly the length of the building itself, awash in an eerie green light, filled with hundreds of bubbling fish tanks.

"Oh my," Clemency gasped. Madame Yi pulled Clemency in and together they began exploring the tanks. In each one, a rare fish moved and floated. Now and then a water mammal, now and then an octopus.

Woolley was oddly appalled by the display. All these sad, beautiful fish alone, harboured in these tanks. It felt almost oppressive.

"Impressive, no?" said Mr. Yu.

The guests all politely agreed.

"Woolley," Clemency whispered, as she walked back over to him. "We must leave now. There is something here. Something heavy. I can't explain it but I cannot take anymore of this show."

Woolley agreed, but knew he had to find a way to exit without letting Mr. Yu feel he had lost face. He walked over to Mr. Yu. "Old chap, I fear Clemency has taken ill…"

"Oh!" chirped Mr. Yu, shooting him a look of terrified concern. "Not something she ate here, I hope. We get our food from reputable sources, not from here! I have my own private practitioner of *Zhōngyī*."

"No, no, Mr. Yu, it's all the excitement. She is just overwhelmed by the magnificence of it all. What she needs is a good night's rest."

Mr. Yu looked deeply hurt, but stiffened. "Of course, Mr. Woolley, we must do what is best for Miss de la Tour. I find western women much more fragile than the Chinese." Clemency bristled. Woolley caught her eye and gave her a 'not now' look.

"I am just so honoured to have been able to show you what little I could of the excitement and high-class entertainment that my humble city Shanghai has to offer. May I give you the use of my car and driver to get you to your establishment safely?"

"Thank you, Mr. Yu, but we cannot impose on you even more."

Mr. Yu smiled. "Think nothing of it." He raised a hand and a sleek gentleman with shining black hair and an equally shiny suit appeared at his side. He whispered to the man, who then looked at them and bowed deeply.

"This is Qian Qing. He is my trusted man and driver, and he will get you to your destination safely."

"Do forgive me, Mr. Yu," said Clemency. "I was having such a lovely time. You've been so courteous in showing us your Shanghai. But I fear it may have been too much for me." Woolley poked Clemency and she gently kicked his ankle.

Qian Qing gestured to the wall. "This way, please." He pressed a section of tapestry and a door opened silently. "Secret passage to hidden garage."

Woolley thanked Mr. Yu again, and then taking Clemency by her arm said, "How very exciting, jumping the queue."

They settled into the large sedan, different than the one that brought them to the restaurant. Small running lights on the door and floor created an amber hue. A fan mounted on the back of the driver's seat oscillated noiselessly, blowing the hot stifling air that had been trapped in the car. Clemency took Woolley's hand. "That was a bit much," she said, exasperated. "I do not want another evening like that. I will never get the image of Woodside-Chang and those girls scraping his ears out of my head."

"Same darling, same. When next we plan a trip, let us leave the word 'adventure' right out of it. And heat. Perhaps there is luxury accommodation in Antarctica. Think of it darling — penguins, iced martinis and you."

The car lurched. "Excuse please," said the driver. "Problem in road."

Woolley and Clemency looked outside. It was unusually dark in this area of the city. They could see sandbags stacked around an overturned car, which in turn was blocking most of the roadway. A number of rickshaw drivers were lined up shouting, showing papers and gesticulating at what looked like Japanese military police. Woolley felt a knot grow in his stomach. "I fear, darling, our evening's adventures are not yet over. Can you make anything out of what is being shouted?"

"Someone is yelling something about a curfew, that if he is late returning his rickshaw, he will have to pay a full day's extra rent for it." Clemency sat back in the car. "Oh Woolley, what is happening?"

Woolley tightened his hand on hers. "This area has always been controlled by the crime syndicate; well, pretty much everything is controlled by the crime syndicate, but this is their home turf. I fear the Japanese are trying to make a point. There have been rumblings for some time."

"Woolley, this is not just a surprise birthday party with my relatives, this is…"

"Darling, I apologize. I have underestimated the current situation and the hunger of Imperial Japan. And because of that I am a tad worried," He stopped and looked into Clemency's eyes.

Suddenly there was the crack of a gun. They looked out of the window to see the man who had been complaining lying gasping in a pool of blood. The other drivers moved off as quickly and silently as they could. Woolley then noticed a rickshaw turning the corner onto the road. The driver immediately took in the situation but the passengers, an American-looking couple in evening dress, seemed oblivious. One of the Japanese officers turned towards the newcomer, and the man, looking down at the body of his fellow driver, immediately lifted his rickshaw bar and ran. The motion caused the conveyance to tilt back, trapping the couple. The man, struggling to maintain his dignity, managed to crawl out, then helped his wife. Looking around for his driver, he saw the Japanese officers and started yelling.

"What did you do with my driver, you goddam yellow lot?" His wife grabbed his arm, calling for composure, but he pulled it away from her. "I am American. I have business here, you goddam monkeys. We need a driver now!" One of the soldiers started walking towards the angry man. "Finally, a goddam foreigner who sees some sense," the American said. The soldier calmly lifted his rifle and pointed it directly at the man's head, then lowered his rifle and walked away laughing. The Americans quickly turned and quietly started walking back the way they had come.

The driver turned and looked at Woolley and Clemency with a determined look. "Hold tight please," he said and turning back, took a deep breath and slammed down hard on the accelerator. With a violent and unexpected lurch, the enormous grey chariot shot forward through the ragged road block and on to safety. The Japanese were too startled to do anything before the car was out of range, so they just shook their fists and shouted.

"The Japanese," the driver said once they were clear enough for him to slow down, "have no right to stop us, not in Shanghai; they are playing with fire."

"Thank you, Mr. Qing," said Clemency in Cantonese. "We owe you our lives."

He bowed his head slightly, still watching the road.

The city now was eerily silent as they crossed into Daphne's concession. Lights were snuffed, windows shuttered. The car eventually stopped in front of the alley that lead down to Daphne's store. The stillness when they got out of the car was unnerving to them both.

"Please be safe returning," Clemency said to Qing.

He smiled. "I have family here, so I am staying. I will not be driving through that again tonight; I might scratch Mr. Yu's car." With a light purr the formidable automobile glided off into the night.

"A drink about now would be lovely," said Woolley.

"For once I would have to agree with you, darling," said Clemency.

Woolley leaned over and kissed Clemency deeply. She

couldn't help but notice as he was holding her that his whole body was shaking.

Chapter 22

They walked down the darkened alley and out into the courtyard near the tea shop. Woolley looked up and could see a million stars all shining, just for them, he thought. He held Clemency close as they walked; he could never tire of her, of her physical being, of her wit and odd brain. "Darling," Woolley said after a moment. "I simply cannot live without you. Terrifying now to think of not being with you. To be without you. We are on this lovely, tiny island with hot and cold running water." He paused. "Darling, I think when we get home, we should get a cat."

"A cat?"

"Yes. A cat."

Clemency tangled her fingers about Woolley's and smiled. "I would like that. Can it be black?"

"Naturally."

They came upon the shop. It was shuttered like all the rest but there was light seeping out of every window. "Don't like the look of this," said Woolley. "I'm hoping it's just our Daphne waiting up for us. Perhaps she brought the whole gang back for a night cap." Clemency rummaged in her clutch for the key Daphne had given them. She handed it to Woolley, who wrestled with it in the lock and finally got it to click open.

"Oh, I am glad this evening's over," sighed Clemency as Woolley threw open the door.

They walked in to see that every light had been turned on in the shop. Daphne was standing with her back to them, rocking softly back and forth.

"Daphne," Clemency said quietly.

Daphne turned quickly, her face ashen, her eyes wide open, black as night. She looked in their direction, but it was if they didn't exist. Suddenly she began to shake violently and was about to scream until her focus returned and she recognized who was standing in front of her.

Clemency rushed forward. "Good lord, Daphne!"

It was then that Benedict stepped into the room. Woolley was about to walk over to him when Benedict lifted his finger to his mouth and quietly set down a large glass full of amber liquid on the bar. He nodded to Woolley to indicate he would be back with two more and left the room as quietly as he entered.

Confused, Woolley and Clemency both took hold of Daphne, unsure what to do. They guided her over to a table and sat down. "There, there," said Woolley uselessly.

"Father and Mother. No heads! Warning… warning!" Daphne kept repeating, over and over.

Woolley looked to Clemency, hoping for some sort of aid. Clemency looked to Woolley, her eyes conveying, "I have no idea."

Woolley got up and grabbed the glass from the bar. He sipped – bourbon – and brought it over to Daphne.

"Shh, shh, here drink this, it will calm you."

Daphne sipped and coughed.

"I'd prefer water," she whispered.

"That is for plants," replied Woolley, thankful that she was back with them, and all three of them smiled.

Benedict then came back into the room, carrying a tray with two full martini glasses and a shaker. He placed it down on the table and moved to one side, slightly away from the table.

"Oh Cecil, Clemency, it was just horrible. Horrible. I was walking home alone when … when …"

"It's okay," said Clemency soothingly. "Just start from the beginning. Well, start when you left your friends."

Daphne took another sip. "It was a usual night. I don't really like bridge, I prefer mahjong, but I have a group of friends, people not from here that I can talk to, and they love to play. It was stifling in the apartment and by the end of the night all I wanted was air. I know it is becoming dangerous to be out alone, but I thought I was safe enough as it wasn't that far, and I know the way blindfolded. The air was heavy and sweet, and I had my bike…" Slowly and hesitantly her story unfolded. Woolley and Clemency sat silently, trying to wrap their heads around what Daphne was telling them.

"Oh Daphne, darling" started Clemency, "I don't know what to say."

Woolley, having downed his drink in one gulp, grabbed the shaker and was set to pour himself another. "Daphne, darling, were you sure it was them? There is strange business going on which all seems to be centred around you and this establishment. Could they have been tricksters?"

"I know what I saw!" she cried.

Woolley cleared his throat. "Then we must find out

why."

"That's just it," sobbed Daphne, "I just don't know why! There is nothing here out of the ordinary. The property is no more valuable than any of the other shops in the square. I did what my parents had requested when they died. Why now? Why me? Did I dishonour them? What have I done wrong?"

"There, there," Woolley put his arms around her gently. "There must be some explanation, some sort of …"

Benedict then stepped forward. "It seems Miss Daphne was not the only one to see the dead tonight."

Benedict proceeded to tell them of his encounter in the alley. But there was more, for when that door had opened, he had seen something that he believed he was not supposed to have seen. "Tomorrow a very auspicious moon enters a very dangerous house. In the light I also saw a man. He seemed to have layers; he was shedding layers. I can't even describe it. Layers of red light just radiated off of him. The light was full of symbols. I began to see it was a map. The man pointed. 'There' he said. 'That is the opening. That is the door.' It took me a moment, but I realized he was showing me a map which led to here, to the shop."

"Could you make anything else out?" asked Woolley.

"It was nothing I had seen before. There were clusters of characters and symbols."

Woolley reached into his inner jacket and pulled out his fountain pen. "Daphne, do you have some paper?" Daphne fetched him some from the register. "Now," he turned to Benedict, "can you write down or draw anything you remember?"

"I was unfamiliar, as I said, with most of it, or all of it. It wasn't traditional Chinese symbols, or any kind of symbols I know of. I have a small knowledge of many written languages: angelic, demonic, Sinhalese, Cyrillic."

"Without a doubt, Benedict, your knowledge is more than just 'small'," said Woolley, with a slight smile.

Benedict picked up the pen and began to scribble, talking as he wrote. "There were a lot of lines, almost like a grid, a map." He drew what he could remember. "It was pointing, leading to here."

Suddenly there was a furious pounding on the shop door. Daphne screamed and Woolley dropped his glass. Benedict got up and proceeded to the door. In Cantonese he shouted, "Who is there?"

"Benedict," came the voice from outside, "it is St. Andrew Woodside-Chang and my daughter. Make haste, open the door, there isn't a moment to lose."

Clemency looked to Woolley, terrified. Woolley was not happy but knew he must allow them access. "Let them in, Benedict."

A dreadful booming came from the direction of the harbour, rattling the shop. When Benedict opened the door, the sky was ablaze in green light illuminating much of the street, silhouetting the buildings in view. Woodside-Chang's great bulk then blocked the entrance. "Nothing's happened yet?" he gasped, out of breath. Akimbad skittered by in front of him and Woodside-Chang yelled, "Lock the door, quickly, lock the door… Ah, wait!" He took out a very delicate mirror and hung it on the front door, then closed it himself, locking it. He turned to the room. "Is everyone all here?"

"What is the meaning of this? Who is everyone?" asked Woolley.

Impatiently Woodside-Chang hissed, "The three of you, dammit, and the daughter Daphne. This will not work if you aren't all present."

"We are all here, but the question is, why are you? And work? What work? What in blazes is going on?"

"In case you haven't realized, Mr. Woolley," Woodside-Chang breathed in loudly, "there is a war on, two wars in fact. One in the harbour… a battle for this puny, pusillanimous city, and one that is about to be played out here for the very world." He paused for effect. "The VERY WORLD!" He dramatically laid onto the table a beaten leather satchel and started pulling out implements. "Is this the largest table you have?" He asked.

"What are you planning on doing?" asked Woolley. "If what you are saying is true, and from what we've learned from Benedict I am fearing the worst, would it not be wiser to make safe the store and let us help you in your preparations?" From the back of the room Akimbad tittered.

The air had become more humid as Woodside-Chang fussed with his bag. There was a noticeable smell of sulphur.

"How so?" Clemency questioned, putting her arms around Daphne.

"Wha…?" grumbled Woodside-Chang.

"Save the world?"

"Don't be thick, woman. You know as well as I what is happening here." He suddenly noticed Benedict's scribbled map. "You have a map? How do you have one? Mr. Yu and I only secured a copy a number of months ago, it was next to impossible to acquire. How do have you one?"

Woolley took it up. "Benedict drew it. He became aware of it tonight."

"Ah, then more is afoot than we feared. Quickly, help me position the table and these articles. I'm sure, Mr. Woolley, you know what they are for?"

"I know they are for a séance. My question to you is, for what purpose? It's very dangerous to attempt something like this in an uncontrolled environment."

"Good g od man, are you thick, also? I am trying to staunch the flow of evil."

Woolley was taken aback. "Sorry old man, I had you written down as playing for the dark side in this drama."

"Sir," said Woodside-Chang, insulted. "I never do good for others. I attend to my own needs. Do what thou will. It just so happens that my needs, Mr. Yu's needs and your needs all coalesce." He continued setting up, laying out a black cloth and drawing a pentagram with white chalk. "It just so happens that Mr. Yu and I uncovered a rather dangerous bit of underworld administrative … business, shall we say. A dangerous bit of business, which if allowed to transpire would be a disaster. Have you heard of the Magnialtacarta?"

"Good g od, the pact of the underworlds," stammered Woolley.

"Yes, indeed. A pact that every 668 years is reviewed for which new terms are drawn up."

Clemency spoke up, "A pact? There is more than one 'underworld.'"

Woodside-Chang barked out a laugh. "Madam, there are two, the East and the West. They do not speak to each other save through scribes and red-tape minions, but the time has come to redress the pact and I have gotten word that the East has something up their sleeve. A demand." He began to hum and continued with his preparation. Woolley, in anxiety, began helping. Woodside-Chang continued, "I am quite happy with my lifestyle and do not want a change to the status quo. It is imperative that I do what I can to help with this ... business."

The floor of the café began to rumble, which had nothing to do with the guns going off in the harbour. "Where the hell is Mr. Yu?" grumbled Woodside-Chang, looking at his watch. Then came a knock. Benedict opened the door and Mr. Yu stormed in. The outside was clouded with smoke.

"A thousand apologies," he said, distracted. "Chang, there is so much to do. Everything is much worse than I thought. I predicted bad, and this is much worse. Are you sure your daughter is strong enough?"

Woodside-Chang gave Mr. Yu a contemptuous glance. "She is flesh of my flesh; she is a rock of strength."

"Please," cried Daphne. "Why here? Why my home? My store? Did I do something wrong at my parents' funeral?"

"Don't be daft, girl!" Woodside Chang roared. "Your parents are bugs. Tiny ants crawling. You are an insect. What is happening here is something so gigantic, even I am humbled by its scope. Your parents just had the misfortune to buy a property affected by the shifting tides of evil. How could they know that 668 years ago this was the site of a kind of administrative building for all of evildom?"

Mr. Yu looked up while adjusting the table. "Very bad chi."

"Akimbad!" cried St. Andrew-Woodside Chang. She had fallen asleep on one of the benches. "Make ready, girl — take off your clothes."

Clemency raced forward. "Now see here, you monster!"

Woodside-Chang looked Clemency up and down pitilessly. "You are a fool, Miss del la Tour, almost as much a fool as Woolley here. But you are both part of this play now, so I must amend. My daughter, who is not a fool, is wearing her ceremonial robe under her pyjamas."

Clemency, insulted, stepped back. Woolley, equally insulted, said, "I will not have you talk to Clemency in that manner."

"Enough Woolley, I haven't time for hurt feelings." There came a tremendous boom from below the floor. "It is beginning. Child, all of us, to the table." Woodside-Chang looked at the gathering. "Akimbad is a very powerful medium. She is a conduit. The dead speak through her and hopefully we will be able to speak to the dead and find out what the Eastern Underworld needs … what it demands." Another boom and from between the floorboards, a green vapour slowly began rising, twisting upwards like strange vines. Woodside-Chang sniffed. "Ha! Clever clogs!"

"Clever clogs?" Mr. Yu asked.

"Our rivals, they are here. Can't you smell them? The mist, they are planning an attack to slow us." He began working impatiently, pulling chairs up to the table, lighting candles. "Woolley, if you please?" Woolley had stopped assisting but now he saw the gravity of the situation and set to helping.

Woodside-Chang stepped back. "We are ready," he snapped as the door blew open and a gush of noxious vapour poured into the room.

Chapter 23

Woolley ran to help Benedict secure the door; once done, each pulled out their handkerchiefs and handed them to Daphne and Clemency. Mr. Yu, Woodside-Chang and the child seemed unaffected. In the green fug, Mr. Yu lit the black candles placed on the table. "Mr. Woolley, please," he said and gestured to a chair. "Chang, you here." Benedict moved forward to sit. "No, please, it must now be a woman. You, Miss de la Tour, please." He pulled out the chair, bowing quickly. Another tremendous boom, which was now augmented with the howling of wind from outside.

"Let us hurry!" shouted Woodside-Chang. "Everyone else, sit now. Daughter, you here."

Akimbad sat at the head of the table, impish and milquetoast in the pale candlelight. She looked down, closing her eyes, then looked up, opening them. They were now black, liquid black. She whispered, "We touch hands. Fingers to fingers. Palms must remain flat. Focus now."

Another loud boom. "Ha!" shouted Woodside-Chang. "It knows. They know!"

"Oh," said Daphne.

"Shush!" Akimbad hissed. The table began to rock

slightly. She pulled the candle closer to her and returned her fingers to the other. She began to chant a low guttural mantra. Woolley stiffened. Clemency made eye contact and Woolley whispered as quietly as he could over the noise, "That is the prayer to invoke the Devil." Woolley looked and could see that Mr. Yu and Woodside-Chang were entranced by the child, her eyes now closed as she swayed slightly side to side. The table bumped on the floor in time with the booming that was increasing frequency below.

"Yes!" Mr Yu shouted. "Hail Satan!"

"Hail Satan," joined Woodside-Chang. "Continue, child!"

Suddenly Akimbad began to rise. Woolley thought she was standing up, but her entire being was rising into the air. Woodside-Chang slowly, quietly began to laugh. Clemency whispered to Woolley, "What is happening?"

"Mediums can lose their earthly weight when they are in a trance and pass it on to the spirit. It's well documented."

Akimbad rose up and uncoiled from her seated position so she was horizontal with the floor. She floated over the table and then rose higher, getting closer and closer to the ceiling fan, stopping just a distance from it. Her form then, without any seen conveyance or effort, moved across the room, floating silently into the back room. Woolley rose up, but Woodside-Chang grabbed his arm. "She is being controlled by forces much greater than you and I." He chortled, "she is in good hands."

Mr. Yu and Woodside-Chang then burst into fanatic laughter. The booming under the floor intensified.

"Good god man, are you sacrificing your daughter?!" Woolley shouted. "I cannot allow that."

Clemency was about to speak when suddenly, silence.

The booming ceased. Even the clock stopped ticking. Daphne put her hands to her ears, fearing she'd been deafened or worse, and began to scream.

"Quiet, girl!" shouted Woodside-Chang. "There is nothing we can do now, it is well and truly begun."

"How correct you are," said a voice, and out from the darkened backroom stepped an elegantly dressed man in smoking jacket and slippers, carrying the girl in his arms.

Both Mr. Yu and Woodside-Chang fell to their knees and began shouting, "Hail Satan, hail Satan!"

The man looked at them unimpressed and gently rested Akimbad on the table. "Well, well," he said, looking around the room, "word must have gotten out." He stepped forward, put ting on a pair of glasses. "Mr. Woolley, we've met before, and Miss de la Tour. How strange, I rarely see anyone more than once a lifetime unless they are in my employ, and here we are all together again." A glass had fallen to the floor. The gentleman reached down and placed it on the table. "And Daphne, charmed." He took her shaking hand. "Child, there is little to fear of me. I do so apologize for the ruckus, but rules are rules. And 667 years ago, when we put this in our schedules, you weren't around to question availability. I just hope there isn't going to be a mess."

Daphne's eyes widened and she stammered, "A m-m-mess?"

"I shouldn't think there will be. We are the civilized ones, but negotiations can get sticky."

"Hail Satan!" shouted Mr. Yu and Woodside-Chang in supplicating unison.

"Enough, please," the man snapped. "We get the picture." The men painfully got to their feet; Woodside-Chang could not hide his elation but in Mr. Yu, he detected fear. Rightly so. The air smelled of ozone and, oddly, of hay.

"And this child," he walked over to the table, waving his hand over Akimbad and straightening her dress. "She is yours, is she not, Moffat St. Andrew Woodside-Chang?"

"Hail Satan!" Woodside-Chang roared. "She is the spawn of the horned one!"

"I'm pretty sure she is yours," said the gentleman, unimpressed. "I have a final say about those matters. Your rumblings make much noise in my administration. Why are you here, by the way?"

"Hail Satan! We've gotten word that the Eastern Underworld has hatched a plan to counter the 'understanding.' We called you to humbly offer our help."

"Come, come, did you think I wouldn't know about this … plan … to counter the understanding, as you put it? And don't flatter yourself, I came on my own accord. This has been in my books for, well, 667 years. I've come prepared."

"Hail Satan!" shouted Mr. Yu and Woodside-Chang and they fell onto their knees again.

Woolley stepped forward. "Look here, this is between you and this other power, correct? Do you really need us to be here? It could get messy and we are, essentially, in the way."

"Hmm," said the gentleman who was now scanning

the shelf of books left out for the café's patrons. He tapped an abnormally long black nail on the spine of The Great Gatsby. "Liked that one. Hmm. Oh, no Mr. Woolley, I cannot let your party go, you are here for the duration. Like it or not, you are part of this bargaining." Woolley felt suddenly ill and stepped back to be with Clemency, Daphne and Benedict.

Woodside-Chang and Mr. Yu had, all this time, been jabbering and chanting in a kind of ecstasy. "Hail Satan! Hail Satan! Hail Satan!" The gentleman looked at them with a hint of sadness and almost pity, and snapped his fingers. Both men instantly turned into a roiling, steaming mess of ordure, maggots and eyeballs.

"Oh my god !" cried Clemency and turned her head, gasping at the stench. Both Woolley and Benedict made to go to the men but realized there was little, if anything, they could do; the horror was done. The entrails writhed gelatinously, and slowly formed into a coil of writhing snakes. No one could take their eyes off the seething pile of flesh and goo. The gentleman smiled. "At long last, silence." Daphne began to sob uncontrollably.

"Now," the gentleman continued, "to business." He reached into his pocket and pulled out a deck of cards. He fanned them out on the table next to Akimbad, who was now jerking slightly and glistening with perspiration, and he randomly pulled one from the spread. Looking at it he said simply, "Ah" and replaced it in the deck. He then, with a sweep of his hands, brought the cards together again into a neatly stacked pile and placed them back into his waistcoat pocket. Then, with his hands he drew a square in the air in front of him, silently incanting.

Woolley was staring, as were they all. Benedict was slowly edging to the door in hopes of gaining a better position. The man, as if reading Benedict's thoughts, snapped his fingers and Benedict froze, paralyzed. The gentleman waved to belay their fears. "He's fine, he's fine."

Where the square was now drawn, a weird green light began to almost seep through the invisible lines. There was a burning odour and then, suddenly a space – a window, a portal, a door – grew out of the nothingness. It widened large enough to allow someone to pass through. From where they were standing, they could not see what was on the other side.

The gentleman stepped back as a regally dressed man in eastern court attire stepped into the room through the opening.

"Who are you?" the gentleman asked with disdain.

The man bowed. "I am Mizi Xia," he said in a calm, measured fashion and bowed again.

"So? Who are you to me?"

"I am the Minister of, how do you say, Corporeal Affairs in the Glorious Kingdom of Shadows."

"You are an executive assistant; he sent an executive assistant."

"Correction please, I am the Minister…"

"You're an assistant. For deuce's sake he's known about this meeting for 667 years; he couldn't have cleared his calendar? I am a very, very, very busy person."

"Humbly, may I remind you of your operating budget: half of the Eastern Kingdom of Shadows. Your domain, may I remind you again please, one quarter the size." He bowed. "Although most certainly as complex, you must understand that …"

"Enough. Where is he?"

"He is here in the form of me, his Proxy; he has granted me power to do and obey and bargain for our next 667 years of tranquil understanding."

"Don't waste my time!" shouted the gentleman who, in his anger, seemed to be growing in size. "This portal must be closed, we must relocate our site of meeting; those idiots there," he gestured to the snakes, "found it, and how many others know? Is there no obligation to silence anymore? We were wrong to be so complacent. I need Cheng Wen here, now, to discuss this."

The messenger bowed and covered his ears, "Do not use the name of the High Emperor, Lord of the Gods, Lord of the Shadows, so casually."

The gentleman smirked, "Lord of the …"

"Might I remind you, with deepest respect, you are not Lord and Master here. This portal was installed millennia ago as a means for the ruling heads to assess the living without the formality of … how do you say … red tape?"

"Well, I want it closed. Surely we can communicate on some other level, some common ground, not here, in this tea shop?" boomed the gentleman.

"Gentlemen," said Woolley, clearing his throat.

The Eastern Minister hissed, "Who is this?" unaware there were others in the room. "Who are all these humans; are they yours?"

"Heavens no. These are bystanders, very much underfoot."

"Shoo them away," the Minister ordered, gesturing

with his hands in a sweeping fashion, though he paused at seeing Clemency.

Woolley tried again. "May I asked, humbly, what …"

"Silence!" shouted the gentleman. "Unfortunately, you are seeing the two greatest, darkest, most brilliant powers involved in a petty pissing contest. An Admin Assistant!"

"Minister of …"

"Assistant! How will closing his portal lessen his power? Is that what he thinks, and then he acts too busy to tell me to my face? If your world wasn't so tied up in ceremony and red tape, I would have a mind…"

The Minister held up a finger. "Dangerous words — please."

The gentleman quieted, and in doing so became his original size. He smoothed his smoking jacket. "I am a reasonable man. Are you in communication with the Emperor? Can he hear us?"

"Oh yes, he is very much aware."

"I figured as much. He's cheated me out of much, but this I will not stand for. Can you ask him his thoughts?"

"He agrees with the idea of closing the portal but feels a fee must be paid. Certain power concessions."

"Power concessions? What in blazes?!" The gentleman collected himself and breathed in. "If I agree to meet in person with my ministers to discuss these concessions, does he give me power, now, right here, to close this portal?"

The Minister paused. "A date must be decided on now, for meeting."

"Ha!" laughed the gentleman. "All right, an auspicious date. How about the 4th?"

"Of what calendar?"

"Any calendar, just send me an invitation and I will be there."

The minister pulled a yellow square of paper with red brushwork from his gown and handed it to the Gentleman, then bowed. The gentleman looked at it, folded it once and put it in the pocket of his waistcoat. "Fine then, anything else?"

The minister smiled, "Yes."

"What then? I've lost my patience for this."

"Humbly, The High Emperor, Lord of the Gods, Lord of the Shadows wants," the Minister turned and pointed at Clemency, "Her."

"No!" Woolley shouted.

"Oh Woolley," cried Clemency as she was suddenly sucked into the darkness and out of sight. Woolley ran fast at the portal, but it became the nothing that it was, just empty space. He fell to his knees in complete and utter, hopeless shock.

The gentleman made a brushing gesture with his hands, and just as he came, left through the backroom door.

Epilogue

Woolley lay back, exhausted. He was still in the evening clothes he was in yesterday. He inhaled a sigh of warm scented air as he settled back onto the bed. Clemency, sleeping on her side, mewed slightly and pressed her back closer to him. "I adore you," she said sleepily, and then fell back to sleep. She was wearing his pyjamas and looked so much better in them, he thought, than he did. She was exquisite perfection to him. Absolutely imperfectly perfect. Where would he be, had he not found this other misfit?

Stone-tired, he slipped his right hand under the band of her pyjama bottoms and began to gently caress her. He moved slowly down her warm silken skin, reading her, each rise and fall, each beat of her heart. He rubbed her buttocks, so in love with her, her very soul, her skin, in love with how some parts were so firm and unforgiving and others so warm and tender. He moved his hand to the small of her back, across her dimples to the perfect triangle that formed at the base of her spine. Lingered there, moved his fingers over it, feeling coarse and unworthy. He then slid upwards, over and around to the magic that were her firm and pronounced hipbones, and down to the sudden and magical oasis of her sparse but perfect pubic hair. Clemency squirmed slightly and rolled onto her back. He twisted his fingers in her hair, an altar of devotion. He moved his hand up in the darkness, trailing the rise of her smoothness to the pucker of her appendix scar, and remembered each time she told the story of it bursting and her father giving her tea. He moved then up her belly, her mole, and felt the strange sensation of sudden, even softer skin under her breasts.

"Woolley," she said, murmuring in her sleep.

"Darling," he said in a whisper so as not to wake her.

"Woolley," she said again, her hands now rocking him.

"Mister Woolley." He opened his eyes, stinging with the acrid stench of the opium pipe. Around him lay, in fantastic disarray, the many men and women attempting to escape their own personal hells. He was stiff from haunted sleep, he felt he had no liquid in him, he was just sinew, nothing more. His head ached. A tiny woman dressed in red, the house mistress, tapped him again and said, "Mister Woolley."

"Yes, what?" mumbled Woolley, disorientated, and it all came crushing back to him.

"Your niece is here, Mister Woolley. She has suitcases. You go now. Mr. Woolley I never say this to anyone, but maybe you should find some other way to not dream. To people who walk with ghosts, the pipe only bring them demons." She turned and quietly said something in Malay dialect to the shadows. A very young girl in an orange silk cheongsam appeared balancing a tray with a small black cup and an earthen pot of tea that smelled remarkably of a barnyard. "I like you Mr. Woolley, but you no come back.

Go with your nice niece and leave your ghosts here

with me, I will watch over them for you."

He stiffly crawled to his feet. He could smell the days' sweat that covered and dried upon him. He had little will to move forward, relying on muscle memory to walk. He wanted to evaporate. Just carrying on seemed impossible. But eventually he was standing. He tried to straighten his clothes, to no avail. He felt his face, like paper, and his stubble, so coarse.

The woman led Woolley to the front parlour, the fresh morning light almost blinding. She pressed into his hand a small coin and a mirror. "Catch train now. You go."

"Yes," he said, pushing back the bead curtain which separated the room from the street, his voice hollow and foreign to him. "Must catch the train."

Acknowledgement

This book was written entirely in the Toronto subway, between the hours of 10 and 11 a.m., Tuesday to Saturday, from Donlands to Dundas West. At that time, I was working two days as a (not very good) chocolatier and three days as a gallery assistant and would sit and furiously scribble longhand into my notebook on the commute. If I didn't get a seat, I wasn't able to write that day. I mention this not to celebrate my power of concentration but to thank my editors Gillian Holmes and Jean Nielsen for their monumental effort in untangling my millions of dropped and dangled threads and weaving them into this book, which I am quite proud of. Thank you.

I would also like to thank Nancy Hall, Taeden Hall and Melissa Hickey for reading over the manuscript and making many very valuable suggestions — as well as finding a missing chapter.

Leading up to writing this, when not making chocolates or hanging art, I spent all my waking hours reading or watching everything I possibly could about the era and locations where I've sent Woolley, Clemency and Benedict. I am indebted to the authors of the books I read (a partial reading list follows). I played a little fast and loose with some dates but made up very little. If anything is amiss, I take full responsibility. I was uncomfortable using the Pidgin dialect spoken by the porters and street workers, however I felt it necessary and used it as accurately and sparingly as I could. Thank you must be given to Christy Thomasson who suggested the name Moffatt St. Andrew Woodside-Chang.

The description of the The Grand World, is a paraphrase of a comment by Josef von Sternberg, whose film *Shanghai Express* I consider a masterpiece.

And finally I would like to thank Nancy Baker and Richard Shallhorn whose never ending kindness, generosity and inspiration has been a constant in my life.

Vicki Baum, *Shanghai '37*, Oxford University Press 1987

Eileen Chang, *Lust, Caution*, Anchor 2007

Yangsze Choo, *The Ghost Bride: A Novel*, William Morrow 2013

Stella Dong, *Shanghai: The Rise and Fall of a Decadent City*, William Morrow 2001

S.R. Gibbons & P. Morican, *World War One*, Longmans 1965

Taras Grescoe, *Shanghai Grand: Forbidden Love and International Intrigue on the Eve of the Second World War*, HarperAvenue 2016

Emily Hahn, *China To Me*, Virago 1987

Tsao Hsueh-Chin, *Dream Of The Red Chamber*, Anchor 1958

International Opium Commission, *Report of the International Opium Commission, Shanghai, China, February 1 to February 26, 1909*

Leo Ou-fan Lee, *Shanghai Modern, The Flowering of a New Urban Culture in China, 1930–1945*, Harvard University Press, 1999

Lynn Pan, *Shanghai Style: Art and Design Between the Wars*, Long River Press 2008

Shao Xunmei, *The Verse of Shao Xunmei*, Homa & Sekey Books 2016

David Keyes is the author of over 15 books including *I Do So Worry For All Those Lost At Sea*, An Imagined Autobiography, and two previous Cecil Herbert Woolley adventures.

He is also a maker of clocks, curios and coffins as well as a composer, designer and photographer. He lives in Toronto with numerous cats.

Follow his adventures on Instagram @marlowghost